ABRACADABRA
& OTHER SATIRES

ABRACADABRA & OTHER SATIRES

JOHN GALSWORTHY

WILDSIDE PRESS

Originally published in 1929.
Published by Wildside Press LLC.
wildsidepress.com | bcmystery.com

CONTENTS

ABRACADABRA

Our families occupied neighbouring houses in the country, and Minna used to hide in the bathroom whenever our governess took us round. She was to us but a symbol of shyness for months before she became a body—a very thin body, with dark, straggly hair, and dark eyes, and very long legs and arms for an eight-year-old. Looking back on her hardihoods from eight to fifteen, I find difficulty in assigning to the bathroom period its full significance, to realise that she actually used to make herself invisible because she could not face strange people even of her own age. She faced us so beautifully afterward, would steal up behind and pull our hairs, and bag our caps and throw them up on to the tops of wardrobes, and then, as likely as not, climb up, throw them down, and follow with a jump. Few were the tops of our trees that did not know her in her blue jersey and red cap, and stockings green at the knees and showing little white portions of her. She had a neck long as a turkey's and feet narrow as canoes. She was certainly going to be tall. Though quite normal about sticking pins into a body, making the lives of calves and dogs burdensome, giving fizzy magnesia to cats, fetching stray souls down with a booby-trap, and other salutary pastimes, she would dissolve into tears and rush away if anybody played Chopin, or caught and killed a butterfly; and, if one merely shot a little bird with a catapult, would dash up and thump him. When she fought she was like a tiger-cat, but afterward would sit and shake uncontrollably with most dreadful dry sobs. So there was no relying on her.

She could not have been called pretty in those days.

She became fifteen and went to school. We saw little of her for three years. At eighteen she came home, and out. Then we would meet her at dances, and picnics, skating and playing tennis—always languid, pale, dark-eyed; still not quite regular in her features, and with angles not perfectly covered; but, on the whole, like a tall lily with a dark centre. She was very earnest, too, and beginning to be æsthetic, given to standing against walls, with her dark-brown eyes immovably fixed on persons playing violins; given to Russian linen and embroidering book covers; to poetry and the sermons of preachers just unorthodox enough; dreamy, too, but puffing and starting at things that came too near. She was very attractive.

Going to college, one saw little more of Minna till she was twenty-two. She was working then at a "Settlement," and looked unhappy and anæmic.

Two months later we were told she had broken down. The work was too painful; her nerves had gone all wrong. She was taken abroad.

We did not see her again till she was twenty-six. She was then marrying a Quaker, a handsome, big fellow with reddish hair, ten years older than herself. More like a swaying lily than ever she looked in her long white veil. A tall, striking couple! The Quaker had warm eyes, and by the way he looked at her, one wondered.

Another four years had passed before I, at all events, saw much of Minna again. She was now thirty, and had three children, two girls and a boy, and was evidently soon to have another. There was a pathetic look in her eyes. They said that the Quaker should have been a Turk, for his physique was powerful and his principles extremely strict. His wife had grown to have a shrinking, fagged-out air, and worried terribly over her infants. She was visibly unhappy; had gone off, too, in looks; grown sallow and thin-cheeked, and seemed not to care to hold herself up.

I recollect the Quaker coming in one day, full of health and happiness, and putting his affectionate hand on her shoulder. To me—not to the Quaker, from whom many things were hidden—it was apparent that she flinched, and when his back was turned I saw in a mirror that she was actually trembling all over, and on her face an expression as if she saw before her suffering from which she could not possibly escape. It was clear that the quivering, lilylike creature had been brought almost to her last gasp by the physique and principles of that healthy, happy Quaker. It was quite painful to see one for whom life seemed so terribly too much.

She was, I think, about thirty-two when one noticed how much better she was looking. She had begun to fill out and hold herself up; her eyes had light in them again. Though she was more attractive than ever, and the Quaker had abated no jot of either principle or physique, she had given up quivering and starting, and had a way of looking tranquilly through or over him, as if he were not there, though her amiability was obviously perfect, and from all accounts she fulfilled every duty better than ever. She no longer worried over her children, of whom there were now five. It was mysterious. I can only describe the impression she made by saying that she seemed in a sort of trance, seeing and listening to something far away. There was a curious intentness in her eyes, and her voice had acquired a slight but not unpleasing drawl, as though what she was talking of had little reality. Every afternoon from three to four she was invisible.

Having in those days a certain interest in psychology, one used to concern oneself to account for the extraordinary change in her that was becoming more marked every year. By the time she was thirty-five it really seemed impossible that she could ever have been a sensitive, high-strung creature, hiding in the bathroom, thumping us for killing butterflies, sobbing afterward so uncontrollably; suffering such tortures from the "Settlement," and the Quaker, and her children, whose ailments and troubles she now supported with an equanimity which any one, seeing her for the first time, would surely have mistaken for callousness. And all the time she was putting on flesh without, however, losing her figure. Indeed, in those days she approached corporeal perfection.

And at last one afternoon I learned the reason.

She no longer believed she had a body!

She told me so, almost with tears of earnestness. And when I pointed out to her humbly that she had never had more, she insisted that I saw nothing really sitting there except the serene and healthy condition of her spirit. Long she talked to me that afternoon, explaining again and again, in her slightly drawling voice, that she could never have gone on but for this faith; and how comforting and uplifting it was, so that no one who lacked it could be really happy! Every afternoon—she told me—from three to four she "held" that idea of "no body."

This was all so startling to me that I went away and thought it over. Next day I came back and said that I did not see how it could be much good to her to have no body, so long as other people still had theirs; since it was their bodies, not hers, which had caused her pain and grief.

"But, of course," she said, "they haven't."

I had just met the Quaker coming in from golf, and could only murmur: "Is that really so?"

"I couldn't bear, now," she said, "to think they had."

"Then, do you really mean, Minna, that when they are there they are not there?"

"Yes!" And her eyes shone.

I thought of her eldest boy, who happened to be ill with mumps.

"What, then, is Willy's mumps," I said, "if not an affection of the fleshy tissue of his cheeks and neck? Why should he cry with pain, and why should he look so horrid?"

She frowned, as if reflecting hard.

"When you came in," she said, "I'd just been holding the thought that he has no body, and I don't—I really don't feel any longer that he has mumps. So I don't worry. And that's splendid both for him and me."

I saw that it was splendid for her; but how was it splendid for him? I did not ask, however, because she looked so earnest and uplifted, and I was afraid of seeming unkind.

The next day I came back again, and said:

"I've been thinking over your faith, Minna. Candidly, I've never seen any one improve so amazingly in health and looks since you've had it. But what I've been wondering is, whether it's in the nature of fresh air, hard work, and plain living, or in the nature of a drug or anodyne. Whether it's prevention, or cure. In fact, whether you could hold it, or ever have held it, unless you had been sick *before* you held it?"

She evidently did not grasp my meaning. I could, of course, have made it plain enough by saying: "Suppose you had not been a self-conscious, self-absorbed, high-strung, anæmic girl, like so many nowadays, quivering at life and Quakers with strong physique and principles; suppose you had been an Italian peasant woman or an English cottage lass, obliged to work and think of others all her time; suppose, in a word, you had not had the chance to be so desperately sensitive and conscious of your body—do you think you would ever have felt the necessity for becoming unconscious of it?" But she looked so serene and puzzled, so corporeally charming on her sofa, that I hadn't the heart to put it thus brutally; and I merely said:

"Do tell me how the idea first came to you?"

"It was put there. It could never have come of its own accord."

"No doubt; but what exactly?"

She grew rather pink.

"It was one evening when Willy—he was only four then—had been very naughty, and Tom" (this was the Quaker) "insisted on my whipping him. I was obliged to, you see, for fear he would do it himself. Poor Willy cried so that I was simply in despair. It hurt me awfully; I remember thinking: 'Ah! but it's not really me; not me—not my arm.' It seemed to me that there was a dreadful unreality about myself; that I was not really doing it, and so I surely could not be hurting him. It was such a comfort—and I wanted comfort."

I felt the sacredness and the pathos of that; I felt, too, that her despair, before that comfort came, had been her farewell to truth; but I would not for the world have said that, nor asked what Willy's tears had really been, if not real tears.

"Yes," I murmured; "and after that?"

"After that—I tried every day, and gradually the whole beauty of it came to me—because, you know, there are so many things to fret one, and it's so splendid to feel uplifted above it all."

They tell me the morphia habit is wonderful! But I only said:

"And so you really never suffer now?"

"Oh!" she answered, "I often have the beginnings; but I just hold that thought and—it goes. I do wish—I *do* wish you would try!"

"Yes, yes," I murmured; "yes, yes!" She looked so pathetically earnest and as if she would be so disappointed. "But just one thing: Don't you ever feel that the knowledge that people have no bodies and don't really suffer——" and there I stopped. I had meant to add—"blunts sympathy and dries up the springs of fellow-feeling from which all kindly action comes?" But I hadn't the heart.

"Oh! do put any questions to me!" she said. "You can't shake my faith! It's religion with me, you know."

"You certainly seem fitter and stronger every day. I quite understand that you're being saved by it. And that's the essence of religion, isn't it?"

She drew herself up and smiled. "Tom says I'm getting fat!"

I looked at her. I must say that, for one who had no body, she was superb.

After that I again left London and did not see her for two years.

A few days after my return I asked after her at my sister's.

"Oh! haven't you heard? The most dreadful tragedy happened there six weeks ago. Kitty and Willy" (they were the two eldest children) "were run over by a motor; poor little Kitty was killed on the spot, and Willy will be lame for life, they say."

Thinking of Kitty blotted out like that—a little thing all shyness, sensibility, and pranks, just as Minna had been at her age—I could scarcely ask: "How does poor Minna take it?"

My sister wrinkled her brows.

"I was there," she said, "when they brought the children in. It was awful to see Tom—he broke down utterly. He's been quite changed ever since."

"But Minna?"

"Minna—yes. I shall never forget the expression of her face that first minute. It reminded me of—I don't know what—like nerves moving under the skin. Dreadful! And then, ten minutes later, it was quite calm; you'd have thought nothing had happened. She's very wonderful. I've watched her since, and I don't—I really don't believe she feels it!"

"How is she looking?"

"Oh! just the same—very well and handsome. Rather too fat."

It was with very curious feelings that I went next day to see Minna. Truly she looked magnificent in her black clothes. Her curves had become ampler, her complexion deeper, perhaps a little coarse, and her drawl was more pronounced. Her husband came in while I was there. The poor man was indeed a changed Quaker. He seemed to have shrivelled. When she put her hand on his shoulder, I noticed with surprise that he jibbed away and seemed to avoid the gaze of her rather short-sighted, beautiful brown eyes that had grown appreciably warmer. It was strange indeed—his body had become so meagre and hers had so splendidly increased! We made no mention of the tragedy while he was there, but when he had left us I hazarded the question:

"How is poor little Willy?"

Her eyes shone, and she said, with a sort of beautiful earnestness:

"You mustn't call him that. He's not a bit unhappy. We hold the thought together. It's coming wonderfully!"

In a sudden outburst of sympathy I said:

"I'm so sorry. It must be terrible for you all."

Her brow contracted just a little.

"Yes! I can't get Tom—if only he would see that it's nothing, really—that there's no such thing as the body. He's simply wearing himself away; he's grown quite thin; he's——" She stopped. And there rose up in me a kind of venom, as if I felt that she was about to say '—no longer fit to be my mate.' And, trying to keep that feeling out of my eyes, I looked at the magnificent creature. How marvellously she had flourished under the spell of her creed! How beautifully preserved and encased against the feelings of this life she had become! How grandly she had cured her sensitive and neurasthenic girlhood! How nobly, against the disease of self-consciousness and self-absorption, she had put on the armour of a subtler and deeper self-absorption!

And suddenly I pitied or I envied her—Ah! which? For, to achieve immunity from her own suffering, I perceived that for the suffering of others she had become incapable of caring two brass buttons.

THE VOICE OF——!

The proprietor of "The Paradise" had said freely that she would "knock them." Broad, full-coloured, and with the clear, swimming eye of an imaginative man, he was trusted when he spoke thus of his new "turns." There was the feeling that he had once more discovered a good thing.

And on the afternoon of the new star's dress rehearsal it was noticed that he came down to watch her, smoking his cigar calmly in the front row of the stalls. When she had finished and withdrawn, the *chef d'orchestre*, while folding up his score, felt something tickling his ear.

"Bensoni, this is hot goods!"

Turning that dim, lined face of his, whose moustache was always coming out of wax, Signor Bensoni answered: "A bit of all right, boss!"

"If they hug her real big tonight, send round to my room."

"I will."

Evening came, and under the gilt-starred dome the house was packed. Rows and rows of serious seekers for amusement; and all the customary crowd of those who "drop in"—old clients with hair and without hair, in evening clothes, or straight from their offices or race-course; bare-necked ladies sitting; ladies who never sat, but under large hats stood looking into the distance, or moved with alacrity in no particular direction, and halted swiftly with a gentle humming; lounging and high-collared youths, furtively or boldly staring, and unconsciously tightening their lips; distinguished goatee-bearded foreigners wandering without rest. And always round the doorways the huge attendants, in their long, closely buttoned coats.

The little Peruvian bears had danced. The Volpo troupe in claret-coloured tights had gone once more without mishap through their hairbreadth tumbles. The Mulligatawny quartet had contributed their "unparalleled plate spray." "Donks, the human ass," had brayed. Signor Bensoni had conducted to its close his "Pot-pourriture" which afforded so many men an opportunity to stretch their legs. Arsenico had swallowed many things with conspicuous impunity. "Great and Small Scratch" had scratched. "Fraulein Tizi, the charming female vocalist," had suddenly removed his stays. There had been no minute dull; yet over the whole performance had hung that advent of the new star, that sense of waiting for a greater moment.

She came at last—in black and her own whiteness, "La Bellissima," straight from Brazil; tall, with raven-dark hair, and her beautiful face as pale as ivory. Tranquilly smiling with eyes only, she seemed to draw the gaze of all into those dark wells of dancing life; and, holding out her arms, that seemed fairer and rounder than the arms of women, she said: "Ladies and gentlemen, I will dance for you de latest Gollywog Brazilian caterpillar crawl."

Then, in lime-light streaming down on her from the centre of the gallery, she moved back to the corner of the stage. Those who were wandering stood still; every face craned forward. For, sidelong, with a mouth widened till it nearly reached her ears, her legs straddling, and her stomach writhing, she was moving incomparably across the stage. Her face, twisted on her neck, at an alarming angle, was distorted to a strange, inimitable hideousness. She reached the wings, and turned. A voice cried out: "Épatant!" Her arms, those round white arms, seemed yellow and skinny now, her obviously slender hips had achieved miraculous importance; each movement of her whole frame was attuned to a perfect harmony of ugliness. Twice she went thus marvellously up and down, in the ever-deepening hush. Then the music stopped, the lime-light ceased to flow, and she stood once more tranquil and upright, beautiful, with her smiling eyes. A roar of enthusiasm broke, salvo after salvo—clapping and "Bravos," and comments flying from mouth to mouth.

"Rippin'!" "Bizarre—I say—how bizarre!" "Of the most chic!" "*Wunderschön!*" "Bully!"

Raising her arms again for silence, she said quite simply: "Good! I will now, ladies and gentlemen, sing you the latest Patagonian Squaw Squall. I sing you first, however, few bars of 'Che farò' old-fashion, to show you my natural tones—so you will see." And in a deep, sweet voice began at once: "Che farò senz' Euridice"; while through the whole house ran a shuffle of preparation for the future. Then all was suddenly still; for from her lips, remarkably enlarged, was issuing a superb cacophony. Like the screeching of parrots, and miauling of tiger-cats fighting in a forest, it forced attention from even the least musical.

Before the first verse was ended, the uncontrollable applause had drowned her; and she stood, not bowing, smiling with her lips now—her pretty lips. Then raising a slender forefinger, she began the second verse. Even more strangely harsh and dissonant, from lips more monstrously disfigured, the great sound came. And, as though in tune with that crescendo, the lime-light brightened till she seemed all wrapped in flame. Before the storm of acclamation could burst from the enraptured house, a voice coming from the gallery was heard suddenly to cry:

"Woman! Blasphemous creature! You have profaned Beauty!"

For a single second there was utter silence, then a huge, angry "Hush!" was hurled up at the speaker; and all eyes turned toward the stage.

There stood the beautiful creature, motionless, staring up into the lime-light. And the voice from the gallery was heard again.

"The blind applaud you; it is natural. But you—unnatural! Go!" The beautiful creature threw up her head, as though struck below the jaw, and with hands flung out, rushed from the stage. Then, amidst the babel of a thousand cries—"Chuck the brute out!" "Throw him over!" "Where's the manager?" "Encore, encore!"—the manager himself came out from the wings. He stood gazing up into the stream of lime-light, and there was instant silence.

"Hullo! up there! Have you got him?"

A voice, far and small, travelled back in answer: "It's no one up here, sir!"

"What? Limes! It was in front of you!" A second faint, small voice came quavering down: "There's been no one hollerin' near me, sir."

"Cut off your light!"

Down came the quavering voice: "I 'ave cut off, sir."

"What?"

"I 'ave cut off—I'm disconnected."

"Look at it!" And, pointing toward the brilliant ray still showering down onto the stage, whence a faint smoke seemed rising, the manager stepped back into the wings.

Then, throughout the house, arose a hustling and a scuffling, as of a thousand furtively consulting; and through it, of it, continually louder, the whisper—"Fire!"

And from every row some one stole out; the women in the large hats clustered, and trooped toward the doors. In five minutes "The Paradise" was empty, save of its officials. But of fire there was none.

Down in the orchestra, standing well away from the centre, so that he could see the stream of lime-light, the manager said:

"Electrics!"

"Yes, sir."

"Cut off every light."

"Right, sir."

With a clicking sound the lights went out; and all was black—but for that golden pathway still flowing down the darkness. For a moment the manager blinked silently at the strange effulgence. Then his scared voice rose: "Send for the Boss—look alive! Where's Limes?"

Close to his elbow a dark little quick-eyed man, with his air of professional stupidity, answered in doubt: "Here, sir."

"It's up to you, Limes!"

The little man, wiping his forehead, gazed at the stream of golden light, powdering out to silver at its edges.

"I've took out me limes, and I'm disconnected, and this blanky ray goes on. What am I to do? There's nothing up there to cause it. Go an' see for yourself, sir!" Then, passing his hand across his mouth, he blurted out: "It's got to do with that there voice—I shouldn't be surprised. Unnat'ral-like; the voice o'——"

The manager interrupted sharply: "Don't be a d—d ass, Limes!"

And, suddenly, all saw the proprietor passing from the prompt side behind that faint mist where the ray fell.

"What's the theatre dark like this for? Why is it empty? What's happened?"

The manager answered.

"We're trying to find out, sir; a madman in the gallery, whom we couldn't locate, made a disturbance, called the new turn 'A natural'; and now there's some hanky with this lime. It's been taken out, and yet it goes on like that!"

"What cleared the house?"

The manager pointed at the stage.

"It looked like smoke," he said. "That light's loose; we can't get hold of its end anywhere."

From behind him Signor Bensoni suddenly pushed up his dim, scared face.

"Boss!" he stammered: "it's the most bizarre—the most bizarre—thing I ever struck—Limes thinks——"

"Yes?" The Boss turned and spoke very quickly: "What does he think—yes?"

"He thinks—the voice wasn't from the gallery—but higher; he thinks—he thinks—it was the voice of—voice of——"

A sudden sparkle lit up the Boss's eyes. "Yes?" he hissed out; "yes?"

"He thinks it was the voice of—— Hullo!"

The stream of light had vanished. All was darkness.

Some one called: "Up with your lights!"

As the lights leaped forth, all about the house, the Boss was seen to rush to the centre of the stage, where the ray had been.

"Bizarre! By gum!... Hullo! Up there!"

No sound, no ray of light, answered that passionately eager shout.

The Boss spun round: "Electrics! You blazing ass! Ten to one but you've cut my connection, turning up the lights like that. The voice of——! Great snakes! What a turn! What a turn! I'd have given it a thou' a week!... *Hullo! up there! Hullo!*"

But there came no answer from under the gilt-starred dome.

A SIMPLE TALE

Talking of anti-Semitism one of those mornings, Ferrand said: "Yes, *monsieur*, plenty of those gentlemen in these days esteem themselves Christian, but I have only once met a Christian who esteemed himself a Jew. *C'était très drôle—je vais vous conter cela.*

"It was one autumn in London, and, the season being over, I was naturally in poverty, inhabiting a palace in Westminster at fourpence the night. In the next bed to me that time there was an old gentleman, so thin that one might truly say he was made of air. English, Scotch, Irish, Welsh—I shall never learn to distinguish those little differences in your race—but I well think he was English. Very feeble, very frail, white as paper, with a long grey beard, and caves in the cheeks, and speaking always softly, as if to a woman.... For me it was an experience to see an individual so gentle in a palace like that. His bed and bowl of broth he gained in sweeping out the kennels of all those sorts of types who come to sleep there every night. There he spent all his day long, going out only at ten hours and a half every night, and returning at midnight less one quarter. Since I had not much to do, it was always a pleasure for me to talk with him; for, though he was certainly a little *toqué*," and Ferrand tapped his temple, "he had great charm, of an old man, never thinking of himself, no more than a fly that turns in dancing all day beneath a ceiling. If there was something he could do for one of those specimens—to sew on a button, clean a pipe, catch beasts in their clothes, or sit to see they were not stolen, even to give up his place by the fire—he would always do it with his smile so white and gentle; and in his leisure he would read the Holy Book! He inspired in me a sort of affection—there are not too many old men so kind and gentle as that, even when they are 'crackey,' as you call it. Several times I have caught him in washing the feet of one of those sots, or bathing some black eye or other, such as they often catch—a man of a spiritual refinement really remarkable; in clothes also so refined that one sometimes saw his skin. Though he had never great thing to say, he heard you like an angel, and spoke evil of no one; but, seeing that he had no more vigour than a swallow, it piqued me much how he would go out like that every night in all the weather at the same hour for so long a promenade of the streets. And when I interrogated him on this, he would only smile his smile of one not there, and did not seem to know very much of what I was talking.

I said to myself: 'There is something here to see, if I am not mistaken. One of these good days I shall be your guardian angel while you fly the night.' For I am a connoisseur of strange things, *monsieur*, as you know; though, you may well imagine, being in the streets all day long between two boards of a sacred sandwich does not give you too strong a desire to *flâner* in the evenings. *Eh, bien!* It was a night in late October that I at last pursued him. He was not difficult to follow, seeing he had no more guile than an egg; passing first at his walk of an old shadow into your St. James's Park along where your military types puff out their chests for the nursemaids to admire. Very slowly he went, leaning on a staff—*une canne de promenade* such as I have never seen, nearly six feet high, with an end like a shepherd's crook or the handle of a sword, a thing truly to make the *gamins* laugh—even me it made to smile though I am too well accustomed to mock at age and poverty, to watch him march in leaning on that cane. I remember that night—very beautiful, the sky of a clear dark, the stars as bright as they can ever be in these towns of our high civilisation, and the leaf-shadows of the plane-trees, colour of grapes on the pavement, so that one had not the heart to put foot on them. One of those evenings when the spirit is light, and policemen a little dreamy and well-wishing. Well, as I tell you, my Old marched, never looking behind him, like a man who walks in sleep. By that big church—which, like all those places, had its air of coldness, far and ungrateful among us others, little human creatures who have built it—he passed, into the great Eaton Square, whose houses ought well to be inhabited by people very rich. There he crossed to lean him against the railings of the garden in the centre, very tranquil, his long white beard falling over hands joined on his staff, in awaiting what—I could not figure to myself at all. It was the hour when your high *bourgeoisie* return from the theatre in their carriages, whose manikins sit, the arms crossed, above horses fat as snails. And one would see through the window some lady *bercée doucement*, with the face of one who has eaten too much and loved too little. And gentlemen passed me, marching for a mouthful of fresh air, *très comme il faut*, their concertina hats pushed up, and nothing at all in their eyes. I remarked my Old, who, making no movement watched them all as they went by, till presently a carriage stopped at a house nearly opposite. At once, then he began to cross the road quickly, carrying his great stick. I observed the lackey pulling the bell and opening the carriage door, and three people coming forth—a man, a woman, a young man. Very high *bourgeoisie*, some judge, knight, mayor—what do I know?—with his wife and son, mounting under the porch. My Old had come to the bottom of the steps, and spoke, in bending himself forward, as if supplicating. At once those three turned their faces, very astonished. Although I was very intrigued, I could not hear what he was saying, for, if I came nearer, I feared he would see me spying on him. Only the sound of his voice I heard, gentle as always; and his hand I saw wiping his forehead, as though he had carried something heavy from very far. Then the lady spoke to her husband, and went into the house, and the young son followed in lighting a cigarette. There rested only that good father of the family, with his grey whiskers and nose a little bent, carrying an expression as if my Old were making him ridiculous. He made a quick gesture, as though he said, 'Go!' then he too fled softly. The door was shut. At once the lackey mounted, the carriage drove away, and all was as if it had never been, except that my Old was, standing there, quite still. But soon he came returning carrying his staff as if it burdened him. And recoiling in a porch to see him pass, I saw his visage full of dolour, of one overwhelmed with fatigue and grief; so that I felt my heart squeeze me. I must well confess, *monsieur*, I was a little shocked to see this old sainted father asking as it seemed for alms. That is a thing I myself have never done, not even in the greatest poverty—one is not like your 'gentlemen'—one does always some little thing for the money he receives, if it is only to show a drunken man where he lives. And I returned in meditating deeply over this problem, which well seemed to me fit for the angels to examine; and knowing what time my Old was always re-entering, I took care to be in my bed before him. He came in as ever, treading softly so as not to wake us others, and his face had again its serenity, a little 'crackey.' As you may well have remarked, *monsieur*, I am not one of those individuals who let everything grow under the nose without pulling them up to see how they are made. For me the greatest pleasure is to lift the skirts of life, to unveil what there is under the surface of things which are not always what they seem, as says your good little poet. For that one must have philosophy, and a certain industry, lacking to all those gentlemen who think they alone are industrious because they sit in chairs and blow into the telephone all day, in filling their pockets with money. Myself, I coin knowledge of the heart—it is the only gold they cannot take from you. So that night I lay awake. I was not content with what I had seen; for I could not imagine why this old man, so unselfish, so like a saint in thinking ever of others, should go thus every night to beg, when he had always in this palace his bed, and that with which to keep his soul within his rags. Certainly we all have our vices, and gentlemen the most revered do, in secret, things they would cough to see others doing; but that business of begging seemed scarcely in his character of an old altruist—for in my experience, *monsieur*, beggars are not less egoist than millionaires. As I say, it piqued me much, and I resolved to follow him again. The second night was of the most different. There was a great wind, and white clouds flying in the moonlight. He commenced his pilgrimage in passing by your House of Commons, as if toward the river. I like much that great river of yours. There is in its career something of very grand; it ought to know many things, although it is so silent, and gives to no one the secrets which are confided to it. He had for objective, it seemed, that long row of houses very respectable, which gives on the embankment, before you arrive at Chelsea. It was painful to see the poor Old, bending almost double against that great wind coming from the west. Not too many carriages down here, and few people—a true wilderness, lighted by tall lamps which threw no shadows, so clear was the moon. He took his part soon, as of the other night, standing on the far side of the road, watching for the return of some lion to his den. And presently I saw one coming, accompanied by three lionesses, all taller than himself. This one was bearded, and carried spectacles—a real head of learning; walking, too, with the step of a man who knows his world. Some professor—I said to myself—with his harem. They gained their house at fifty paces from my Old; and, while this learned one was opening the door, the three ladies lifted their noses in looking at the moon. A little of æsthetic, a little of science—as always with that type there! At once I had perceived my Old coming across, blown by the wind like a grey stalk of thistle; and his face, with its expression of infinite pain as if carrying the sufferings of the world. At the moment they see him those three ladies drop their noses, and fly within the house as if he were the pestilence, in crying, 'Henry!' And out comes my *monsieur* again, in his beard and spectacles. For me, I would freely have given my ears to hear, but I saw that this good Henry had his eye on me, and I did not budge, for fear to seem in conspiracy. I heard him only say: 'Impossible! Impossible! Go to the proper place!' and he shut the door. My Old remained, with his long staff resting on a shoulder bent as if that stick were of lead. And presently he commenced to march again whence he had come, curved and trembling, the very shadow of a man, passing me, too, as if I were the air. That time also I regained my bed before him, in meditating very deeply, still more uncertain of the psychology of this affair, and resolved once again to follow him, saying to myself: 'This time I shall run all risks to hear.' There are two kinds of men in this world, *monsieur*, one who will not rest content till he has become master of all the toys that make a fat existence—in never looking to see of what they are made; and the other, for whom life is tobacco and a crust of bread, and liberty to take all to pieces, so that his spirit may feel good within him. Frankly I am of that kind. I rest never till I have found out why this is that; for me mystery is the salt of life, and I must well eat of it. I put myself again, then, to following him the next night. This time he traversed those little dirty streets of your great Westminster, where all is mixed in a true pudding of lords and poor wretches at two sous the dozen; of cats and policemen; kerosene flames, abbeys, and the odour of fried fish. Ah! truly it is frightful to see your low streets in London; that gives me a conviction of hopelessness such as I have never caught elsewhere; piquant, too, to find them so near to that great House which sets example of good government to all the world. There is an irony so ferocious there, *monsieur*, that one can well hear the good God of your *bourgeois* laugh in every wheel that rolls, and the cry of each cabbage that is sold; and see him smile in the smoky light of every flare, and in the candles of your cathedral, in saying to himself: 'I have well made this world. Is there not variety here?— *en voilà une bonne soupe!*' This time, however, I attended my Old like his very shadow, and could hear him sighing as he marched, as if he also found the atmosphere of those streets too strong. But all of a sudden he turned a corner, and we were in the most quiet, most beautiful little street I have seen in all your London. It was of small, old houses, very regular, which made as if they inclined themselves in their two rows before a great church at the end, grey in the moonlight, like a mother. There was no one in that street, and no more cover than hair on the head of a pope. But I had some confidence now that my Old would not remark me standing there so close, since in these pil-grimages he seemed to remark nothing. Leaning on his staff, I tell you he had the air of an old bird in a desert, reposing on one leg by a dry pool, his soul looking for water. It gave me that notion one has sometimes in watching the rare spectacles of life—that sentiment which, according to me, pricks artists to their work. We had not stayed there too long before I saw a couple march-ing from the end of the street, and thought: 'Here they come to their nest.' Vigorous and gay they were, young married ones, eager to get home; one could see the white neck of the young wife, the white shirt of the young man, gleaming under their cloaks. I know them well, those young couples in great cities, without a care, taking all things, the world before them, *très amou-reux*, without, as yet, children; jolly and pathetic, having life still to learn— which, believe me, *monsieur*, is a sad enough affair for nine rabbits out of ten. They stopped at the house next to where I stood; and, since my Old was coming fast as always to the feast, I put myself at once to the appearance of ringing the bell of the house before me. This time I had well the chance of hearing. I could see, too, the faces of all three, because I have by now the habit of seeing out of the back hair. The pigeons were so anxious to get to their nest that my Old had only the time to speak, as they were in train to vanish. 'Sir, let me rest in your doorway!' *Monsieur*, I have never seen a face so hopeless, so crippled with fatigue, yet so full of a gentle dignity as that of my Old while he spoke those words. It was as if something looked from his visage surpassing what belongs to us others, so mortal and so cynic as human life must well render all who dwell in this earthly paradise. He held his long staff upon one shoulder, and I had the idea, sinister enough, that it was crush-ing his body of a spectre down into the pavement. I know not how the im-pression came, but it seemed to me that this devil of a stick had the nature of a heavy cross reposing on his shoulder; I had pain to prevent myself turning, to find if in truth 'I had them' as your drunkards say. Then the young man called out: 'Here's a shilling for you, my friend!' But my old did not budge, answering always: 'Sir, let me rest in your doorway!' As you may well imagine, *monsieur*, we were all in the silence of astonishment, I pulling away at my bell next door, which was not ringing, seeing I took care it did not; and those two young people regarding my Old with eyes round as moons, out of their pigeon-house, which I could well see was prettily feathered. Their hearts were making seesaw, I could tell; for at that age one is still impressionable. Then the girl put herself to whispering, and her husband said those two words of your young 'gentlemen,' 'Awfully sorry!' and put out his hand, which held now a coin large as a saucer. But again my Old only said: 'Sir, let me rest in your doorway!' And the young man drew back his hand quickly as if he were ashamed, and saying again, 'Sorry!' he shut the door. I have heard many sighs in my time—they are the good little accompaniments to the song we sing, we others who are in poverty; but the sigh my Old pushed then—how can I tell you—had an accent as if it came from Her, the faithful companion, who marches holding the hands of men and women so that they may never make the grand mistake to imagine themselves for a moment the good God. Yes, *monsieur*, it was as if pursued by Suffering herself, that bird of the night, never tired of flying in this world where they talk always of cutting her wings. Then I took my resolution, and, coming gently from behind, said: 'My Old—what is it? Can I do anything for you?' Without looking at me, he spoke as to himself: 'I shall never find one who will let me rest in his doorway. For my sin I shall wander forever!' At this moment, *monsieur*, there came to me an inspiration so clear that I marvelled I had not already had it a long time before. He thought himself the Wandering Jew! I had well found it. This was certainly his fixed idea, of a cracked old man! And I said: 'My Jew, do you know this? In doing what you do, you have become as Christ, in a world of wandering Jews!' But he did not seem to hear me, and only just as we arrived at our palace became again that old gentle being, thinking never of himself."

Behind the smoke of his cigarette, a smile curled Ferrand's red lips under his long nose a little on one side.

"And, if you think of it, *monsieur*, it is well like that. Provided there exists always that good man of a Wandering Jew, he will certainly have become as Christ, in all these centuries of being refused from door to door. Yes, yes, he must well have acquired charity the most profound that this world has ever seen, in watching the crushing virtue of others. All those gentry, of whom he asks night by night to let him rest in their doorways, they tell him where to go, how to *ménager* his life, even offer him money, as I had seen; but, to let him rest, to trust him in their houses—this strange old man—as a fellow, a brother voyager—that they will not; it is hardly in the character of good citizens in a Christian country. And, as I have indicated to you, this Old of mine, cracked as he was, thinking himself that Jew who refused rest to the good Christ, had become, in being refused for ever, the most Christ-like man I have ever encountered on this earth, which, according to me, is composed almost entirely of those who have themselves the character of the Wandering Jew."

Puffing out a sigh of smoke, Ferrand added: "I do not know whether he continued to pursue his idea, for I myself took the road next morning, and I have never seen him since."

ULTIMA THULE

Ultima Thule! The words come into my head this winter night. That is why I write down the story, as I know it, of a little old friend.

I used to see him first in Kensington Gardens, where he came in the afternoons, accompanied by a very small girl. One would see them silent before a shrub or flower, or with their heads inclined to heaven before a tree, or leaning above water and the ducks, or stretched on their stomachs watching a beetle, or on their backs watching the sky. Often they would stand holding crumbs out to the birds, who would perch about them, and even drop on their arms little white marks of affection and esteem. They were admittedly a noticeable couple. The child, who was fair-haired and elfinlike, with dark eyes and a pointed chin, wore clothes that seemed somewhat hard put to it. And, if the two were not standing still, she went along pulling at his hand, eager to get there; and, since he was a very little light old man, he seemed always in advance of his own feet. He was garbed, if I remember, in a daverdy brown overcoat and broad-brimmed soft grey hat, and his trousers, what was visible of them, were tucked into half-length black gaiters which tried to join with very old brown shoes. Indeed, his costume did not indicate any great share of prosperity. But it was his face that riveted attention. Thin, cherry-red, and wind-dried as old wood, it had a special sort of brightness, with its spikes and waves of silvery hair, and blue eyes that seemed to shine. Rather mad, I used to think. Standing by the rails of an enclosure, with his withered lips pursed and his cheeks drawn in till you would think the wind might blow through them, he would emit the most enticing trills and pipings, exactly imitating various birds.

Those who rouse our interest are generally the last people we speak to, for interest seems to set up a kind of special shyness; so it was long before I made his acquaintance. But one day by the Serpentine, I saw him coming along alone, looking sad, but still with that queer brightness about him. He sat down on my bench with his little dried hands on his thin little knees, and began talking to himself in a sort of whisper. Presently I caught the words: "God cannot be like us." And for fear that he might go on uttering such precious remarks that were obviously not intended to be heard, I had either to go away or else address him. So, on an impulse, I said:

"Why?"

He turned without surprise.

"I've lost my landlady's little girl," he said. "Dead! And only seven years old."

"That little thing! I used to watch you."

"Did you? Did you? I'm glad you saw her."

"I used to see you looking at flowers, and trees, and those ducks."

His face brightened wistfully. "Yes; she was a great companion to an old man like me." And he relapsed into his contemplation of the water. He had a curious, precise way of speaking, that matched his pipchinesque little old face. At last he again turned to me those blue youthful eyes that seemed to shine out of a perfect little nest of crow's-feet.

"We were great friends! But I couldn't expect it. Things don't last, do they?" I was glad to notice that his voice was getting cheerful. "When I was in the orchestra at the Harmony Theatre, it never used to occur to me that some day I shouldn't play there any more. One felt like a bird. That's the beauty of music, sir. You lose yourself; like that blackbird there." He imitated the note of a blackbird so perfectly that I could have sworn the bird started.

"Birds and flowers! Wonderful things; wonderful! Why, even a butter-cup——!" He pointed at one of those little golden flowers with his toe. "Did you ever see such a marvellous thing?" And he turned his face up at me. "And yet, somebody told me once that they don't agree with cows. Now can that be? I'm not a countryman—though I was born at Kingston."

"The cows do well enough on them," I said, "in my part of the world. In fact, the farmers say they like to see buttercups."

"I'm glad to hear you say that. I was always sorry to think they disagreed."

When I got up to go, he rose, too.

"I take it as very kind of you," he said, "to have spoken to me."

"The pleasure was mine. I am generally to be found hereabouts in the afternoons any time you like a talk."

"Delighted," he said; "delighted. I make friends of the creatures and flowers as much as possible, but they can't always make us understand." And after we had taken off our respective hats, he reseated himself, with his hands on his knees.

Next time I came across him standing by the rails of an enclosure, and, in his arms, an old and really wretched-looking cat.

"I don't like boys," he said, without preliminary of any sort. "What do you think they were doing to this poor old cat? Dragging it along by a string to drown it; see where it's cut into the fur! I think boys despise the old and weak!" He held it out to me. At the ends of those little sticks of arms the beast looked more dead than alive; I had never seen a more miserable creature.

"I think a cat," he said, "is one of the most marvellous things in the world. Such a depth of life in it."

And, as he spoke, the cat opened its mouth as if protesting at that assertion. It *was* the sorriest-looking beast.

"What are you going to do with it?"

"Take it home: it looks to me as if it might die."

"You don't think that might be more merciful?"

"It depends; it depends. I shall see. I fancy a little kindness might do a great deal for it. It's got plenty of spirit. I can see from its eye."

"May I come along with you a bit?"

"Oh!" he said; "delighted."

We walked on side by side, exciting the derision of nearly every one we passed—his face looked so like a mother's when she is feeding her baby!

"You'll find this'll be quite a different cat tomorrow," he said. "I shall have to get in, though, without my landlady seeing; a funny woman! I have two or three strays already."

"Can I help in any way?"

"Thank you," he said. "I shall ring the area bell, and as she comes out below I shall go in above. She'll think it's boys. They *are* like that."

"But doesn't she do your rooms, or anything?"

A smile puckered his face. "I've only one; I do it myself. Oh, it'd never do to have her about, even if I could afford it. But," he added, "if you're so kind as to come with me to the door, you might engage her by asking where Mr. Thompson lives. That's me. In the musical world my name was Moronelli; not that I have Italian blood in me, of course."

"And shall I come up?"

"Honoured; but I live very quietly."

We passed out of the gardens at Lancaster Gate, where all the house-fronts seem so successful, and out of it into a little street that was extremely like a grubby child trying to hide under its mother's skirts. Here he took a newspaper from his pocket and wrapped it round the cat.

"She's a funny woman," he repeated; "Scotch descent, you know." Suddenly he pulled an area bell and scuttled up the steps.

When he had opened the door, however, I saw before him in the hall a short, thin woman dressed in black, with a sharp and bumpy face. Her voice sounded brisk and resolute.

"What have you got there, Mr. Thompson?"

"Newspaper, Mrs. March."

"Oh, indeed! Now, you're not going to take that cat upstairs!"

The little old fellow's voice acquired a sudden shrill determination. "Stand aside, please. If you stop me, I'll give you notice. The cat is going up. It's ill, and it is going up."

It was then I said:

"Does Mr. Thompson live here?"

In that second he shot past her, and ascended.

"That's him," she said; "and I wish it wasn't, with his dirty cats. Do you want him?"

"I do."

"He lives at the top." Then, with a grudging apology: "I can't help it; he tries me—he's very trying."

"I am sure he is."

She looked at me. The longing to talk that comes over those who answer bells all day, and the peculiar Scottish desire to justify oneself, rose together in that face which seemed all promontories dried by an east wind.

"Ah!" she said; "he is. I don't deny his heart; but he's got no sense of anything. Goodness knows what he hasn't got up there. I wonder I keep him. An old man like that ought to know better; half-starving himself to feed them." She paused, and her eyes, that had a cold and honest glitter, searched me closely.

"If you're going up," she said, "I hope you'll give him good advice. He never lets me in. I wonder I keep him."

There were three flights of stairs, narrow, clean, and smelling of oilcloth. Selecting one of two doors at random, I knocked. His silvery head and bright, pinched face were cautiously poked out.

"Ah!" he said; "I thought it might be her!"

The room, which was fairly large, had a bare floor with little on it save a camp-bed and chest of drawers with jug and basin. A large bird-cage on the wall hung wide open. The place smelt of soap and a little of beasts and birds. Into the walls, whitewashed over a green wall-paper which stared through in places, were driven nails with their heads knocked off, onto which bits of wood had been spiked, so that they stood out as bird-perches high above the ground. Over the open window a piece of wire netting had been fixed. A little spirit-stove and an old dressing-gown hanging on a peg completed the accoutrements of a room which one entered with a certain diffidence. He had not exaggerated. Besides the new cat, there were three other cats and four birds, all—save one, a bullfinch—invalids. The cats kept close to the walls, avoiding me, but wherever my little old friend went, they followed him with their eyes. The birds were in the cage, except the bullfinch, which had perched on his shoulder.

"How on earth," I said, "do you manage to keep cats and birds in one room?"

"There is danger," he answered, "but I have not had a disaster yet. Till their legs or wings are mended, they hardly come out of the cage; and after that they keep up on my perches. But they don't stay long, you know, when they're once well. That wire is only put over the window while they're mending; it'll be off tomorrow, for this lot."

"And then they'll go?"

"Yes. The sparrow first, and then the two thrushes."

"And this fellow?"

"Ask him," he said. "Would *you* go, bully?" But the bullfinch did not deign to answer.

"And were all those cats, too, in trouble?"

"Yes," he said. "They wouldn't want me if they weren't."

Thereupon he began to warm some blue-looking milk, contemplating the new cat, which he had placed in a round basket close to the little stove, while the bullfinch sat on his head. It seemed time to go.

"Delighted to see you, sir," he said, "any day." And, pointing up at the bullfinch on his head, he added: "Did you ever see anything so wonderful as that bird? The size of its heart! Really marvellous!"

To the rapt sound of that word marvellous, and full of the memory of his mysterious brightness while he stood pointing upward to the bird perched on his thick, silvery hair, I went.

The landlady was still at the bottom of the stairs, and began at once: "So you found him! I don't know why I keep him. Of course, he was kind to my little girl." I saw tears gather in her eyes.

"With his cats and his birds, I wonder I keep him! But where would he go? He's no relations, and no friends—not a friend in the world, I think! He's a character. Lives on air—feeding them cats! I've no patience with them, eating him up. He never lets me in. Cats and birds! I wonder I keep him. Losing himself for those rubbishy things! It's my belief he was always like that; and that's why he never got on. He's no sense of anything."

And she gave me a shrewd look, wondering, no doubt, what the deuce I had come about.

I did not come across him again in the gardens for some time, and went at last to pay him a call. At the entrance to a mews just round the corner of his grubby little street, I found a knot of people collected round one of those bears that are sometimes led through the less conspicuous streets of our huge towns. The yellowish beast was sitting up in deference to its master's nod, uttering little grunts, and moving its uplifted snout from side to side, in the way bears have. But it seemed to be extracting more amusement than money from its audience.

"Let your bear down off its hind legs and I'll give you a penny." And suddenly I saw my little old friend under his flopping grey hat, amongst the spectators, all taller than himself. But the bear's master only grinned and prodded the animal in the chest. He evidently knew a good thing when he saw it.

"I'll give you twopence to let him down."

Again the bear-man grinned. "More!" he said, and again prodded the bear's chest. The spectators were laughing now.

"Threepence! And if you don't let him down for that, I'll hit you in the eye."

The bear-man held out his hand. "All a-right," he said, "threepence; I let him down."

I saw the coins pass and the beast dropping on his forefeet; but just then a policeman coming in sight, the man led his bear off, and I was left alone with my little old friend.

"I wish I had that poor bear," he said; "I could teach him to be happy. But, even if I could buy him, what could I do with him up there? She's such a funny woman."

He looked quite dim, but brightened as we went along.

"A bear," he said, "is really an extraordinary animal. What wise little eyes he has! I do think he's a marvellous creation! My cats will have to go without their dinner, though. I was going to buy it with that threepence."

I begged to be allowed the privilege.

"Willingly!" he said. "Shall we go in here? They like cod's head best."

While we stood waiting to be served I saw the usual derisive smile pass over the fishmonger's face. But my little old friend by no means noticed it; he was too busy looking at the fish. "A fish is a marvellous thing, when you come to think of it," he murmured. "Look at its scales. Did you ever see such mechanism?"

We bought five cod's heads, and I left him carrying them in a bag, evidently lost in the anticipation of five cats eating them.

After that I saw him often, going with him sometimes to buy food for his cats, which seemed ever to increase in numbers. His talk was always of his strays, and the marvels of creation, and that time of his life when he played the flute at the Harmony Theatre. He had been out of a job, it seemed, for more than ten years; and, when questioned, only sighed and answered: "Don't talk about it, please!"

His bumpy landlady never failed to favour me with a little conversation. She was one of those women who have terrific consciences, and terrible grudges against them.

"I never get out," she would say.

"Why not?"

"Couldn't leave the house."

"It won't run away!"

But she would look at me as if she thought it might, and repeat:

"Oh! I never get out."

An extremely Scottish temperament.

Considering her descent, however, she was curiously devoid of success, struggling on apparently from week to week, cleaning, and answering the bell, and never getting out, and wondering why she kept my little old friend; just as he struggled on from week to week, getting out and collecting strays, and discovering the marvels of creation, and finding her a funny woman. Their hands were joined, one must suppose, by that dead child.

One July afternoon, however, I found her very much upset. He had been taken dangerously ill three days before.

"There he is," she said; "can't touch a thing. It's my belief he's done for himself, giving his food away all these years to those cats of his. I shooed 'em out today, the nasty creatures; they won't get in again."

"Oh!" I said, "you shouldn't have done that. It'll only make him miserable."

She flounced her head up. "Hoh!" she said; "I wonder I've kept him all this time, with his birds and his cats dirtying my house. And there he lies, talking gibberish about them. He made me write to a Mr. Jackson, of some theatre or other—I've no patience with him. And that little bullfinch all the time perching on his pillow, the dirty little thing! I'd have turned it out, too, only it wouldn't let me catch it."

"What does the doctor say?"

"Double pneumonia—caught it getting his feet wet, after some stray, I'll be bound. I'm nursing him. There has to be some one with him all the time."

He was lying very still when I went up, with the sunlight falling across the foot of his bed, and, sure enough, the bullfinch perching on his pillow. In that high fever he looked brighter than ever. He was not exactly delirious, yet not exactly master of his thoughts.

"Mr. Jackson! He'll be here soon. Mr. Jackson! He'll do it for me. I can ask him, if I die. A funny woman. I don't want to eat; I'm not a great eater—I want my breath, that's all."

At sound of his voice the bullfinch fluttered off the pillow and flew round and round the room, as if alarmed at something new in the tones that were coming from its master.

Then he seemed to recognise me. "I think I'm going to die," he said; "I'm very weak. It's lucky, there's nobody to mind. If only he'd come soon. I wish"—and he raised himself with feeble excitement—"I wish you'd take that wire off the window; I want my cats. She turned them out. I want him to promise me to take them, and bully-boy, and feed them with my money, when I'm dead."

Seeing that excitement was certainly worse for him than cats, I took the wire off. He fell back, quiet at once; and presently, first one and then another cat came stealing in, till there were four or five seated against the walls. The moment he ceased to speak the bullfinch, too, came back to his pillow. His eyes looked most supernaturally bright, staring out of his little, withered-up old face at the sunlight playing on his bed; he said just audibly: "Did you ever see anything more wonderful than that sunlight? It's really marvellous!" After that he fell into a sort of doze or stupor. And I continued to sit there in the window, relieved, but rather humiliated, that he had not asked me to take care of his cats and bullfinch.

Presently there came the sound of a motorcar in the little street below. And almost at once the landlady appeared. For such an abrupt woman, she entered very softly.

"Here he is," she whispered.

I went out and found a gentleman, perhaps sixty years of age, in a black coat, buff waistcoat, gold watch-chain, light trousers, patent-leather boots, and a wonderfully shining hat. His face was plump and red, with a glossy grey moustache; indeed, he seemed to shine everywhere, save in the eyes, which were of a dull and somewhat liverish hue.

"Mr. Jackson?"

"The same. How is the little old chap?"

Opening the door of the next room, which I knew was always empty, I beckoned Mr. Jackson in.

"He's really very ill; I'd better tell you what he wants to see you about."

He looked at me with that air of "You can't get at me—whoever you may be," which belongs to the very successful.

"Right-o!" he said. "Well?"

I described the situation. "He seems to think," I ended, "that you'll be kind enough to charge yourself with his strays, in case he should die."

Mr. Jackson prodded the unpainted wash-stand with his gold-headed cane.

"Is he really going to kick it?"

"I'm afraid so; he's nothing but skin, bone, and spirit, as it is."

"H'm! Stray cats, you say, and a bird! Well, there's no accounting. He was always a cracky little chap. So that's it! When I got the letter I wondered what the deuce! We pay him his five quid a quarter regular to this day. To tell truth, he deserved it. Thirty years he was at our shop; never missed a night. First-rate flute he was. He ought never to have given it up, though I always thought it showed a bit of heart in him. If a man don't look after number one, he's as good as gone; that's what I've always found. Why, I was no more than he was when I started. Shouldn't have been worth a plum if I'd gone on his plan, that's certain." And he gave that profound chuckle which comes from the very stomach of success. "We were having a rocky time at the Harmony; had to cut down everything we could—music, well, that came about first. Little old Moronelli, as we used to call him—old Italian days before English names came in, you know—he was far the best of the flutes; so I went to him and said: 'Look here, Moronelli, which of these other boys had better go?' 'Oh!' he said—I remember his funny little old mug now—'has one of them to go, Mr. Jackson? Timminsa'—that was the elder—'he's a wife and family; and Smetoni'—Smith, you know—'he's only a boy. Times are bad for flutes.' 'I know it's a bit hard,' I said, 'but this theatre's goin' to be run much cheaper; one of 'em's got to get.' 'Oh!' he said, 'dear me!' he said. What a funny little old chap it was! Well—what do you think? Next day I had his resignation. Give you my word I did my best to turn him. Why, he was sixty then if he was a day—at sixty a man don't get jobs in a hurry. But, not a bit of it! All he'd say was: 'I shall get a place all right!' But that's it, you know—he never did. Too long in one shop. I heard by accident he was on the rocks; that's how I make him that allowance. But that's the sort of hopeless little old chap he is—no idea of himself. Cats! Why not? I'll take his old cats on; don't you let him worry about that. I'll see to his bird, too. If I can't give 'em a better time than ever they have here, it'll be funny!" And, looking round the little empty room, he again uttered that profound chuckle: "Why, he was with us at the Harmony thirty years—that's time, you know; I made my fortune in it."

"I'm sure," I said, "it'll be a great relief to him."

"Oh! Ah! That's all right. You come down to my place"—he handed me a card: "Mr. Cyril Porteus Jackson, Ultima Thule, Wimbledon"—"and see how I fix 'em up. But if he's really going to kick it, I'd like to have a look at the little old chap, just for old times' sake."

We went, as quietly as Mr. Jackson's bright boots would permit, into his room, where the landlady was sitting gazing angrily at the cats. She went out without noise, flouncing her head as much as to say: "Well, now you can see what I have to go through, sitting up here. I never get out."

Our little old friend was still in that curious stupor. He seemed unconscious, but his blue eyes were not closed, staring brightly out before them at things we did not see. With his silvery hair and his flushed frailty, he had an unearthly look. After standing perhaps three minutes at the foot of the bed, Mr. Jackson whispered:

"Well, he does look queer. Poor little old chap! You tell him from me I'll look after his cats and birds; he needn't worry. And now, I think I won't keep the car. Makes me feel a bit throaty, you know. Don't move; he might come to."

And, leaning all the weight of his substantial form on those bright and creaking toes, he made his way to the door, flashed at me a diamond ring, whispered hoarsely: "So long! That'll be all right!" and vanished. And soon I heard the whirring of his car and just saw the top of his shiny hat travelling down the little street.

Some time I sat on there, wanting to deliver that message. An uncanny vigil in the failing light, with those five cats—yes, five at least—lying or sitting against the walls, staring like sphinxes at their motionless protector. I could not make out whether it was he in his stupor with his bright eyes that fascinated them, or the bullfinch perched on his pillow, whom they knew perhaps might soon be in their power. I was glad when the landlady came up and I could leave the message with her.

When she opened the door to me next day at six o'clock I knew that he was gone. There was about her that sorrowful, unmistakable importance, that peculiar mournful excitement, which hovers over houses where death has entered.

"Yes," she said, "he went this morning. Never came round after you left. Would you like to see him?"

We went up.

He lay, covered with a sheet, in the darkened room. The landlady pulled the window-curtains apart. His face, as white now almost as his silvery head, had in the sunlight a radiance like that of a small, bright angel gone to sleep. No growth of hair, such as comes on most dead faces, showed on those frail cheeks that were now smooth and lineless as porcelain. And on the sheet above his chest the bullfinch sat, looking into his face.

The landlady let the curtains fall, and we went out.

"I've got the cats in here"—she pointed to the room where Mr. Jackson and I had talked—"all ready for that gentleman when he sends. But that little bird, I don't know what to do; he won't let me catch him, and there he sits. It makes me feel all funny."

It had made me feel all funny, too.

"He hasn't left the money for his funeral. Dreadful, the way he never thought about himself. I'm glad I kept him, though." And, not to my astonishment, she suddenly began to cry.

A wire was sent to Mr. Jackson, and on the day of the funeral I went down to 'Ultima Thule,' Wimbledon, to see if he had carried out his promise.

He had. In the grounds, past the vinery, an outhouse had been cleaned and sanded, with cushions placed at intervals against the wall, and a little trough of milk. Nothing could have been more suitable or luxurious.

"How's that?" he said. "I've done it thoroughly." But I noticed that he looked a little glum.

"The only thing," he said, "is the cats. First night they seemed all right; and the second, there were three of 'em left. But today the gardener tells me there's not the ghost of one anywhere. It's not for want of feeding. They've had tripe, and liver, and milk—as much as ever they liked. And cod's heads, you know—they're very fond of them. I must say it's a bit of a disappointment to me."

As he spoke, a sandy cat which I perfectly remembered, for it had only half its left ear, appeared in the doorway, and stood, crouching, with its green eyes turned on us; then, hearing Mr. Jackson murmur, "Puss, puss!" it ran for its life, slinking almost into the ground, and vanished among some shrubs.

Mr. Jackson sighed. "Perversity of the brutes!" he said. He led me back to the house through a conservatory full of choice orchids. A gilt bird-cage was hanging there, one of the largest I had ever seen, replete with every luxury the heart of bird could want.

"Is that for the bullfinch?" I asked him.

"Oh!" he said; "didn't you know? The little beggar wouldn't let himself be caught, and the second morning, when they went up, there he lay on the old chap's body, dead. I thought it was very touchin'. But I kept the cage hung up for you to see that I should have given him a good time here. Oh, yes, 'Ultima Thule' would have done him well!"

And from a bright leather case Mr. Jackson offered me a cigar.

The question I had long been wishing to ask him slipped out of me then:

"Do you mind telling me why you called your house 'Ultima Thule'?"

"Why?" he said. "Found it on the gate. Think it's rather distingué, don't you?" and he uttered his profound chuckle.

"First-rate. The whole place is the last word in comfort."

"Very good of you to say so," he said. "I've laid out a goodish bit on it. A man must have a warm corner to end his days in. 'Ultima Thule,' as you say—it isn't bad. There's success about it, somehow."

And with that word in my ears, and in my eyes a vision of the little old fellow in *his* 'Ultima Thule,' with the bullfinch lying dead on a heart that had never known success, I travelled back to town.

STUDIES OF EXTRAVAGANCE

I.—The Writer

Every morning when he awoke his first thought was: How am I? For it was extremely important that he should be well, seeing that when he was not well he could neither produce what he knew he ought, nor contemplate that lack of production with equanimity. Having discovered that he did not ache anywhere, he would say to his wife: "Are you all right?" and, while she was answering, he would think: "Yes—if I make that last chapter pass subjectively through Blank's personality, then I had better——" and so on. Not having heard whether his wife were all right, he would get out of bed and do that which he facetiously called "abdominable cult," for it was necessary that he should digest his food and preserve his figure, and while he was doing it he would partly think: "I am doing this well," and partly he would think: "That fellow in *The Parnassus* is quite wrong—he simply doesn't see——" And pausing for a moment with nothing on, and his toes level with the top of a chest of drawers, he would say to his wife: "What I think about that *Parnassus* fellow is that he doesn't grasp the fact that my books——" And he would not fail to hear her answer warmly: "Of course he doesn't; he's a perfect idiot." He would then shave. This was his most creative moment, and he would soon cut himself and utter a little groan, for it would be needful now to find to find his special cotton wool and stop the bleeding, which was a paltry business and not favourable to the flight of genius. And if his wife, taking advantage of the incident, said something which she had long been waiting to say, he would answer, wondering a little what it was she had said, and thinking: "There it is, I get no time for steady thought."

Having finished shaving he would bathe, and a philosophical conclusion would almost invariably come to him just before he douched himself with cold—so that he would pause, and call out through the door: "You know, I think the supreme principle——" And while his wife was answering, he would resume the drowning of her words, having fortunately remembered just in time that his circulation would suffer if he did not douse himself with cold while he was still warm. He would dry himself, dreamily developing that theory of the universe and imparting it to his wife in sentences that seldom had an end, so that it was not necessary for her to answer them. While dressing he would stray a little, thinking: "Why can't I concentrate myself on my work; it's awful!" And if he had by any chance a button off, he would present himself rather unwillingly, feeling that it was a waste of his time. Watching her frown from sheer self-effacement over her button-sewing, he would think: "She is wonderful! How can she put up with doing things for me all day long?" And he would fidget a little, feeling in his bones that the postman had already come.

He went down always thinking: "Oh, hang it! this infernal post taking up all my time!" And as he neared the breakfast-room, he would quicken his pace; seeing a large pile of letters on the table, he would say automatically: "Curse!" and his eyes would brighten. If—as seldom happened—there were not a green-coloured wrapper enclosing mentions of him in the press, he would murmur: "Thank God!" and his face would fall.

It was his custom to eat feverishly, walking a good deal and reading about himself, and when his wife tried to bring him to a sense of his disorder he would tighten his lips without a word and think: "I have a good deal of self-control."

He seldom commenced work before eleven, for, though he always intended to, he found it practically impossible not to dictate to his wife things about himself, such as how he could not lecture here; or where he had been born; or how much he would take for this; and why he would not consider that; together with those letters which began:

"My dear ——,

"Thanks tremendously for your letter about my book, and its valuable criticism. Of course, I think you are quite wrong.... You don't seem to have grasped.... In fact, I don't think you ever quite do me justice....

"Yours affectionately,
"——."

When his wife had copied those that might be valuable after he was dead, he would stamp the envelopes and, exclaiming: "Nearly eleven—my God!" would go somewhere where they think.

It was during those hours when he sat in a certain chair with a pen in his hand that he was able to rest from thought about himself; save, indeed, in those moments, not too frequent, when he could not help reflecting: "That's a fine page—I have seldom written anything better"; or in those moments, too frequent, when he sighed deeply and thought: "I am not the man I was." About half-past one, he would get up, with the pages in his hand, and, seeking out his wife, would give them to her to read, remarking: "Here's the wretched stuff, no good at all"; and, taking a position where he thought she could not see him, would do such things as did not prevent his knowing what effect the pages made on her. If the effect were good he would often feel how wonderful she was; if it were not good he had at once a chilly sensation in the pit of his stomach, and ate very little lunch.

When, in the afternoons, he took his walks abroad, he passed great quantities of things and people without noticing, because he was thinking deeply on such questions as whether he were more of an observer or more of an imaginative artist; whether he were properly appreciated in Germany; and particularly whether one were not in danger of thinking too much about oneself. But every now and then he would stop and say to himself: "I really must see more of life, I really must take in more fuel"; and he would passionately fix his eyes on a cloud, or a flower, or a man walking, and there would instantly come into his mind the thought: "I have written twenty books—ten more will make thirty—that cloud is grey"; or: "That fellow X—— is jealous of me! This flower is blue"; or: "This man is walking very—very—— D—n *The Morning Muff*, it always runs me down!" And he would have a sort of sore, beaten feeling, knowing that he had not observed those things as accurately as he would have wished to.

During these excursions, too, he would often reflect impersonally upon matters of the day, large questions of art, public policy, and the human soul; and would almost instantly find that he had always thought this or that; and at once see the necessity for putting his conclusion forward in his book or in the press, phrasing it, of course, in a way that no one else could; and there would start up before him little bits of newspaper with these words on them: "No one, perhaps, save Mr. ——, could have so ably set forth the case for Baluchistan"; or, "In *The Daily Miracle* there is a noble letter from that eminent writer, Mr. ——, pleading against the hyperspiritualism of our age."

Very often he would say to himself, as he walked with eyes fixed on things that he did not see: "This existence is not healthy. I really must get away and take a complete holiday, and not think at all about my work; I am getting too self-centred." And he would go home and say to his wife: "Let's go to Sicily, or Spain, or somewhere. Let's get away from all this, and just live." And when she answered: "How jolly!" he would repeat, a little absently: "How jolly!" considering what would be the best arrangement for forwarding his letters. And if, as sometimes happened, they *did* go, he would spend almost a whole morning living, and thinking how jolly it was to be away from everything; but toward the afternoon he would feel a sensation as though he were a sofa that had been sat on too much, a sort of subsidence very deep within him. This would be followed in the evening by a disinclination to live; and that feeling would grow until on the third day he received his letters, together with a green-coloured wrapper enclosing some mentions of himself, and he would say: "Those fellows—no getting away from them!" and feel irresistibly impelled to sit down. Having done so he would take up his pen, not writing anything, indeed—because of the determination to "live," as yet not quite extinct—but comparatively easy in his mind. On the following day he would say to his wife: "I believe I can work here." And she would answer, smiling: "That's splendid"; and he would think: "She's wonderful!" and begin to write.

On other occasions, while walking the streets or about the countryside, he would suddenly be appalled at his own ignorance, and would say to himself: "I know simply nothing—I must read." And going home he would dictate to his wife the names of a number of books to be procured from the library. When they arrived he would look at them a little gravely and think: "By Jove! Have I got to read those?" and the same evening he would take one up. He would not, however, get beyond the fourth page, if it were a novel, before he would say: "Muck! He can't write!" and would feel absolutely stimulated to take up his own pen and write something that was worth reading. Sometimes, on the other hand, he would put the novel down after the third page, exclaiming: "By Jove! He can write!" And there would rise within him such a sense of dejection at his own inferiority that he would feel simply compelled to try to see whether he really was inferior.

But if the book were not a novel he sometimes finished the first chapter before one or two feelings came over him: Either that what he had just read was what he had himself long thought—that, of course, would be when the book was a good one; or that what he had just read was not true, or at all events debatable. In each of these events he found it impossible to go on reading, but would remark to his wife: "This fellow says what I've always said"; or, "This fellow says so and so, now I say——" and he would argue the matter with her, taking both sides of the question, so as to save her all unnecessary speech.

There were times when he felt that he absolutely must hear music, and he would enter the concert-hall with his wife in the pleasurable certainty that he was going to lose himself. Toward the middle of the second number, especially if it happened to be music that he liked, he would begin to nod; and presently, on waking up, would get a feeling that he really was an artist. From that moment on he was conscious of certain noises being made somewhere in his neighbourhood causing a titillation of his nerves favourable to deep and earnest thoughts about his work. On going out his wife would ask him: "Wasn't the Mozart lovely?" or, "How did you like the Strauss?" and he would answer: "Rather!" wondering a little which was which; or he would look at her out of the corner of his eye and glance secretly at the programme to see whether he had really heard them, and which Strauss it might be.

He was extremely averse to being interviewed, or photographed, and all that sort of publicity, and only made exceptions in most cases because his wife would say to him: "Oh! I think you ought"; or because he could not bear to refuse anybody anything; together, perhaps, with a sort of latent dislike of waste, deep down in his soul. When he saw the results he never failed to ejaculate: "Never again! No, really—never again! The whole thing is wrong and stupid!" And he would order a few copies.

For he dreaded nothing so much as the thought that he might become an egoist, and, knowing the dangers of his profession, fought continually against it. Often he would complain to his wife: "I don't think of you enough." And she would smile and say: "Don't you?" And he would feel better, having confessed his soul. Sometimes for an hour at a time he would make really heroic efforts not to answer her before having really grasped what she had said; and to check a tendency, that he sometimes feared was growing on him, to say: "What?" whether he had heard or no. In truth, he was not (as he often said) constitutionally given to small talk. Conversation that did not promise a chance of dialectic victory was hardly to his liking; so that he felt bound in sincerity to eschew it, which sometimes caused him to sit silent for "quite a while," as the Americans have phrased it. But once committed to an argument he found it difficult to leave off, having a natural, if somewhat sacred, belief in his own convictions.

His attitude to his creations was, perhaps, peculiar. He either did not mention them, or touched on them, if absolutely obliged, with a light and somewhat disparaging tongue; this did not, indeed, come from any real distrust of them, but rather from a superstitious feeling that one must not tempt Providence in the solemn things of life. If other people touched on them in the same way, he had, not unnaturally, a feeling of real pain, such as comes to a man when he sees an instance of cruelty or injustice. And, though something always told him that it was neither wise nor dignified to notice outrages of this order, he would mutter to his wife: "Well, I suppose it *is* true—I can't write"; feeling, perhaps, that—if *he* could not with decency notice such injuries, she might. And, indeed, she did, using warmer words than even he felt justified, which was soothing.

After tea it was his habit to sit down a second time, pen in hand; not infrequently he would spend those hours divided between the feeling that it was his duty to write something and the feeling that it was his duty not to write anything if he had nothing to say; and he generally wrote a good deal; for deep down he was convinced that if he did not write he would gradually fade away till there would be nothing left for him to read and think about, and, though he was often tempted to believe and even to tell his wife that fame was an unworthy thing, he always deferred that pleasure, afraid, perhaps, of too much happiness.

In regard to the society of his fellows he liked almost anybody, though a little impatient with those, especially authors, who took themselves too seriously; and there were just one or two that he really could not stand, they were so obviously full of jealousy, a passion of which he was naturally intolerant and had, of course, no need to indulge in. And he would speak of them with extreme dryness—nothing more, disdaining to disparage. It was, perhaps, a weakness in him that he found it difficult to accept adverse criticism as anything but an expression of that same yellow sickness; and yet there were moments when no words would adequately convey his low opinion of his own powers. At such times he would seek out his wife and confide to her his conviction that he was a poor thing, no good at all, without a thought in his head; and while she was replying: "Rubbish! You know there's nobody to hold a candle to you," or words to that effect, he would look at her tragically, and murmur: "Ah! you're prejudiced!" Only at such supreme moments of dejection, indeed, did he feel it a pity that he had married her, seeing how much more convincing her words would have been if he had not.

He never read the papers till the evening, partly because he had not time, and partly because he so seldom found anything in them. This was not remarkable, for he turned their leaves quickly, pausing, indeed, naturally, if there were any mention of his name; and if his wife asked him whether he had read this or that he would answer: "No," surprised at the funny things that seemed to interest her.

Before going up to bed he would sit and smoke. And sometimes fancies would come to him, and sometimes none. Once in a way he would look up at the stars, and think: "What a worm I am! This wonderful Infinity! I must get more of it—more of it into my work; more of the feeling that the whole is marvellous and great, and man a little clutch of breath and dust, an atom, a straw, a nothing!"

And a sort of exaltation would seize on him, so that he knew that if only he did get that into his work, as he wished to, as he felt at that moment that he could, he would be the greatest writer the world had ever seen, the greatest man, almost greater than he wished to be, almost too great to be mentioned in the press, greater than Infinity itself—for would he not be Infinity's creator? And suddenly he would check himself with the thought: "I must be careful— I must be careful. If I let my brain go at this time of night, I sha'n't write a decent word tomorrow!"

And he would drink some milk and go to bed.

II.—The Critic

He often thought: "This is a dog's life! I must give it up, and strike out for myself. If I can't write better than most of these fellows, it'll be very queer." But he had not yet done so. He had in his extreme youth published fiction, but it had never been the best work of which he was capable—it was not likely that it could be, seeing that even then he was constantly diverted from the ham-bone of his inspiration by the duty of perusing and passing judgment on the work of other men.

If pressed to say exactly why he did not strike out for himself, he found it difficult to answer, and what he answered was hardly as true as he could have wished; for, though truthful, he was not devoid of the instinct of self-preservation. He could hardly, for example, admit that he preferred to think what much better books he could have written if only he had not been handicapped, to actually striking out and writing them. To believe this was an inward comfort not readily to be put to the rude test of actual experience. Nor would it have been human of him to acknowledge a satisfaction in feeling that he could put in their proper places those who had to an extent, as one might say, retarded his creative genius by compelling him to read their books. But these, after all, were but minor factors in his long hesitation, for he was not a conceited or malicious person. Fundamentally, no doubt, he lived what he called "a dog's life" with pleasure, partly because he was used to it—and what a man is used to he is loath to part with; partly because he really had a liking for books; and partly because to be a judge is better than to be judged. And no one could deny that he had a distinctly high conception of his functions. He had long laid down for himself certain leading principles of professional conduct, from which he never departed, such as that a critic must not have any personal feelings, or be influenced by any private considerations whatever. This, no doubt, was why he often went a little out of his way to be more severe than usual with writers whom he suspected of a secret hope that personal acquaintanceship might incline him to favour them. He would, indeed, carry that principle further, and, where he had, out of an impersonal enthusiasm at some time or another, written in terms of striking praise, he would make an opportunity later on of deliberately taking that writer down a peg or two lower than he deserved, lest his praise might be suspected of having been the outcome of personal motives, or of gush—for which he had a great abhorrence. In this way he preserved a remarkably pure sense of independence; a feeling that he was master in his own house, to be dictated to only by a proper conviction of his own importance. It is true that there were certain writers whom, for one reason or another, he could not very well stand; some having written to him to point out inaccuracies, or counter one of his critical conclusions, or, still worse, thanked him for having seen exactly what they had meant—a very unwise and even undignified thing to do, as he could not help thinking; others, again, having excited in him a natural dislike by their appearance, conduct, or manner of thought, or by having, perhaps, acquired too rapid or too swollen a reputation to be, in his opinion, good for them. In such cases, of course, he was not so unhuman as to disguise his convictions. For he was, before all things, an Englishman with a very strong belief in the freest play for individual taste. But of almost any first book by an unknown author he wrote with an impersonality which it would have been difficult to surpass.

Then there was his principle that one must never be influenced in judging a book by anything one has said of a previous book by the same writer—each work standing entirely on its own basis. He found this important and made a point of never rereading his own criticisms; so that the rhythm of his judgment, which, if it had risen to a work in 1920, would fall over the author's next in 1921, was entirely unbiassed by recollection, and followed merely those immutable laws of change and the moon so potent in regard to tides and human affairs.

For sameness and consistency he had a natural contempt. It was the unexpected both in art and criticism that he particularly looked for; anything being, as he said, preferable to dulness—a sentiment in which he was supported by the public; not that, to do him justice, this weighed with him, for he had a genuine distrust of the public, as was proper for one sitting in a seat of judgment. He knew that there were so-called critics who had a kind of formula for each writer, as divines have sermons suitable to certain occasions. For example: "We have in 'The Mazy Swim' another of Mr. Hyphen Dash's virile stories.... We can thoroughly recommend this pulsating tale, with its true and beautiful character study of Little Katie, to every healthy reader as one of the best that Mr. Hyphen Dash has yet given us." Or: "We cannot say that 'The Mazy Swim' is likely to increase Mr. Hyphen Dash's reputation. It is sheer melodrama, such as we are beginning to expect from this writer.... The whole is artificial to a degree.... No sane reader will, for a moment, believe in Little Katie." Toward this sort of thing he showed small patience, having noticed with some acumen a relationship between the name of the writer, the politics of the paper, and the temper of the criticism. No! For him, if criticism did not embody the individual mood and temper of the critic, it was not worthy of the name.

But the canon which of all he regarded as most sacred was this: A critic must surrender himself to the mood and temper of the work he is criticising, take the thing as it is with his own special method and technique, its own point of view, and, only when all that is admitted, let his critical faculty off the chain. He was never tired of insisting on this, both to himself and others, and never sat down to a book without having it firmly in his mind. Not infrequently, however, he found that the author was, as it were, wilfully employing a technique or writing in a mood with which he had no sympathy, or had chosen a subject obviously distasteful, or a set of premises that did not lead to the conclusion which he would have preferred. In such cases his scrupulous honesty warned him not to compromise with his conscience, but to say outright that it would have been better if the technique of the story had been objective instead of subjective; that the morbidity of the work prevented serious consideration of a subject which should never have been chosen; or that he would ever maintain that the hero was too weak a character to be a hero, and the book, therefore, of little interest. If any one pointed out to him that had the hero been a strong character there would have been no book, it being, in point of fact, the study of a weak character, he would answer: "That may be so, but it does not affect what I say—the book would have been better and more important if it had been the study of a strong character." And he would take the earliest opportunity of enforcing his recorded criticism that the hero was no hero, and the book no book to speak of. For, though not obstinate, he was a man who stood to his guns. He took his duty to the public very seriously, and felt it, as it were, a point of honour never to admit himself in the wrong. It was so easy to do that and so fatal; and the fact of being anonymous, as on the whole he preferred to be, made it all the harder to abstain (on principle and for the dignity of criticism) from noticing printed contradictions to his conclusions.

In spite of all the heart he put into his work, there were times when, like other men, he suffered from dejection, feeling that the moment had really come when he must either strike out for himself into creative work, or compile a volume of synthetic criticism. And he would say: "None of us fellows are doing any constructive critical work; no one nowadays seems to have any conception of the first principles of criticism." Having talked that theory out thoroughly he would feel better, and next day would take an opportunity of writing: "We are not like the academic French, to whom the principles of criticism are so terribly important; our genius lies rather in individual judgments, pliant and changing as the works they judge."

There was that in him which, like the land from which he sprang, could ill brook control. He approved of discipline, but knew exactly where it was deleterious to apply it to himself; and no one, perhaps, had a finer and larger conception of individual liberty. In this way he maintained the best traditions of a calling whose very essence was superiority. In course of conversation he would frequently admit, being a man of generous calibre, that the artist, by reason of long years of devoted craftsmanship, had possibly the most intimate knowledge of his art, but he would not fail to point out, and very wisely, that there was no such unreliable testimony as that of experts, who had an axe to grind, each of his own way of doing things; for comprehensive views of literature seen in due perspective there was nothing—he thought—like the trained critic, rising superior, as it were professionally, to myopia and individual prejudice.

Of the new school who maintained that true criticism was but reproduction in terms of sympathy, and just as creative as the creative work it reproduced, he was a little impatient, not so much on the ground that to make a model of a mountain was not quite the same thing as to make the mountain;

but because he felt in his bones that the true creativeness of criticism (in which he had a high belief) was its destructive and satiric quality; its power of reducing things to rubbish and clearing them away, ready for the next lot. Instinct, fortified by his own experience, had guided him to that conclusion. Possibly, too, the conviction, always lurking deep within him, that the time was coming when he would strike out for himself and show the world how a work of art really should be built, was in some sort responsible for the necessity he felt to keep the ground well cleared.

He was nearly fifty when his clock chimed, and he began seriously to work at the creation of that masterpiece which was to free him from "a dog's life," and, perhaps, fill its little niche in the gallery of immortality. He worked at it happily enough till one day, at the end of the fifth month, he had the misfortune to read through what he had written. With his critical faculty he was able to perceive that which gave him no little pain—every chapter, most pages, and many sentences destroyed the one immediately preceding. He searched with intense care for that coherent thread which he had suspected of running through the whole. Here and there he seemed to come on its track, then it would vanish. This gave him great anxiety.

Abandoning thought for the moment, he wrote on. He paused again toward the end of the seventh month, and once more patiently reviewed the whole. This time he found four distinct threads that did not seem to meet; but still more puzzling was the apparent absence of any individual flavour. He was staggered. Before all he prized that quality, and throughout his career had fostered it in himself. To be unsapped in whim or fancy, to be independent, had been the very salt of his existence as a critic. And now, and now— when his hour had struck, and he was in the very throes of that long-deferred creation, to find——! He put thought away again, and doggedly wrote on.

At the end of the ninth month, in a certain exaltation, he finished; and slowly, with intense concentration, looked at what he had produced from beginning to end. And as he looked something clutched at him within and he felt frozen. The thing did not move, it had no pulse, no breath, no colour—it was dead.

And sitting there before that shapeless masterpiece, still-born, without a spirit or the impress of a personality, a horrid thought crept and rattled in his brain. Had he, in his independence, in his love of being a law unto himself, *become so individual that he had no individuality left*? Was it possible that he had judged, and judged, and—not been judged, too long? It was not true—not true! Locking the soft and flavourless thing away, he took up the latest novel sent him, and sat down to read it. But, as he read, the pages of his own work would implant themselves above those that he turned and turned. At last he put the book down, and took up pen to review it. "This novel," he wrote, "is that most pathetic thing, the work of a man who has burned the lamp till the lamp has burned him; who has nourished and cultured his savour, and fed his idiosyncrasies, till he has dried and withered, without savour left." And, having written that damnation of the book that was not his own, the blood began once more flowing in his veins, and he felt warm.

III.—The Plain Man

He was plain. It was his great quality. Others might have graces, subtleties, originality, fire, and charm; they had not his plainness. It was that which made him so important, not only in his country's estimation, but in his own. For he felt that nothing was more valuable to the world than for a man to have no doubts, and no fancies, but to be quite plain about everything. And the knowledge that he was looked up to by the press, and pulpit, and the politician sustained him in the daily perfecting of that unique personality which he shared with all other plain men. In an age which bred so much that was freakish and peculiar, to know that there was always himself with his sane and plain outlook to fall back on, was an extraordinary comfort to him. He knew that he could rely on his own judgment, and never scrupled to give it to a public which never tired of asking for it.

In literary matters especially was it sought for, as invaluable. Whether he had read an author or not, he knew what to think of him. For he had in his time unwittingly lighted on books before he knew what he was doing. They had served him as fixed stars forever after; so that if he heard any writer spoken of as "advanced," "erotic," "socialistic," "morbid," "pessimistic," "tragic," or what not unpleasant, he knew exactly what he was like, and thereafter only read him by accident. He liked a healthy tale, preferably of love or of adventure (of detective stories he was, perhaps, fondest), and insisted upon a happy ending, for, as he very justly said, there was plenty of unhappiness in life without gratuitously adding to it, and as to "ideas," he could get all he wanted and to spare from the papers. He deplored altogether the bad habit that literature seemed to have of seeking out situations which explored the recesses of the human spirit or of the human institution. As a plain man he felt this to be unnecessary. He himself was not conscious of having these recesses, or perhaps too conscious, knowing that if he once began to look, there would be no end to it; nor would he admit the use of staring through the plain surface of society's arrangements. To do so, he thought, greatly endangered, if it did not altogether destroy, those simple faculties which men required for the fulfilment of the plain duties of everyday life, such as: Item, the acquisition and investment of money; item, the attendance at church and maintenance of religious faith; item, the control of wife and children; item, the serenity of nerves and digestion; item, contentment with things as they were.

For there was just that difference between him and all those of whom he strongly disapproved, that whereas *they* wanted to *see* things as they were, *he* wanted to *keep* things as they were. But he would not for a moment have admitted this little difference to be sound, since his instinct told him that he himself saw things as they were better than ever did such cranky people. If a human being had got to get into spiritual fixes, as those fellows seemed to want one to believe, then certainly the whole unpleasant matter should be put into poetry, and properly removed from comprehension. "And, anyway," he would say: "In real life, I shall know it fast enough when I get there, and I'm not going to waste my time nosin' it over beforehand." His view of literary and, indeed, all art, was that it should help him to be cheerful. And he would make a really extraordinary outcry if amongst a hundred cheerful plays and novels he inadvertently came across one that was tragic. At once he would write to the papers to complain of the gloomy tone of modern literature; and the papers, with few exceptions, would echo his cry, because he was the plain man, and took them in. "What on earth," he would remark, "is the good of showin' me a lot of sordid sufferin'? It doesn't make me any happier. Besides"—he would add—"it isn't art. The function of art is beauty." Some one had told him this, and he was very emphatic on the point, going religiously to any show where there was a great deal of light and colour. The shapes of women pleased him, too, up to a point. But he knew where to stop; for he felt himself, as it were, the real censor of the morals of his country. When the plain man was shocked it was time to suppress the entertainment, whether play, dance, or novel. Something told him that he, beyond all other men, knew what was good for his wife and children. He often meditated on that question coming in to the City from his house in Surrey; for in the train he used to see men reading novels, and this stimulated his imagination. Essentially a believer in liberty, like every Englishman, he was only for putting down a thing when it offended his own taste. In speaking with his friends on this subject, he would express himself thus: "These fellows talk awful skittles. Any plain man knows what's too hot and what isn't. All this 'flim-flam' about art, and all that, is beside the point. The question simply is: Would you take your wife and daughters? If not, there's an end of it, and it ought to be suppressed." And he would think of his own daughters, very nice, and would feel sure. Not that he did not himself like a "full-blooded" book, as he called it, provided it had the right moral and religious tone. Indeed, a certain kind of fiction which abounded in descriptions "of her lovely bosom" often struck him pink, as he hesitated to express it; but there was never in such masterpieces of emotion any nasty subversiveness, or wrong-headed idealism, but frequently the opposite.

Though it was in relation to literature and drama, perhaps, that his quality of plainness was most valuable, he felt the importance of it, too, in regard to politics. When they had all done "messing about," he knew that they would come to him, because, after all, there he was, a plain man wanting nothing but his plain rights, not in the least concerned with the future, and Utopia, and all that, but putting things to the plain touchstone: "How will it affect me?" and forming his plain conclusions one way or the other. He felt, above all things, each new penny of the income tax before they put it on, and saw to it if possible that they did not. He was extraordinarily plain about that, and about national defence, which instinct told him should be kept up to the mark at all costs. But there must be ways, he felt, of doing the latter without having recourse to the income tax, and he was prepared to turn out any government that went on lines unjust to the plainest principles of property. In matters of national honour he was even plainer, for he never went into the merits of the question, knowing, as a simple patriot, that his country must be right; or that, if not right, it would never do to say she wasn't. So aware were statesmen and the press of this sound attitude of his mind, that, without waiting to ascertain it, they acted on it in perfect confidence.

In regard to social reform, while recognising, of course, the need for it, he felt that, in practice, one should do just as much as was absolutely necessary and no more; a plain man did not go out of his way to make quixotic efforts, but neither did he sit upon a boiler till he was blown up.

In the matter of religion he regarded his position as the only sound one, for however little in these days one could believe and all that, yet, as a plain man, he did not for a moment refuse to go to church and say he was a Christian; on the contrary, he was rather more particular about it than formerly, since when a spirit has departed, one must be very careful of the body, lest it fall to pieces. He continued, therefore, to be a churchman—living in Hertfordshire.

He often spoke of science, medical or not, and it was his plain opinion that these fellows all had an axe to grind; for *his* part he only believed in them just in so far as they benefited a plain man. The latest sanitary system, the best forms of locomotion and communication, the newest antiseptics, and time-saving machines—of all these, of course, he made full use; but as to the researches, speculations, and theories of scientists—to speak plainly, they were, he thought, "pretty good rot."

He abominated the word "humanitarian." No plain man wanted to inflict suffering, especially on himself. He would be the last person to do any such thing, but the plain facts of life must be considered, and convenience and property duly safeguarded. He wrote to the papers perhaps more often on this subject than on any other, and was gratified to read in their leading articles continual allusion to himself: "The plain man is not prepared to run the risks which a sentimental treatment of this subject would undoubtedly involve"; "After all, it is to the plain man that we must go for the sanity and common sense of this matter." For he had no dread in life like that of being called a sentimentalist. If an instance of cruelty came under his own eyes he was as much moved as any man, and took immediate steps to manifest his disapproval. To act thus on his feelings was not at all his idea of being sentimental. But what he could not stand was making a fuss about cruelties, as people called them, which had not actually come under his own plain vision; to be indignant in regard to such *was* sentimental, he was sure, involving as it did an exercise of imagination, than which there was nothing he distrusted more. Some deep instinct no doubt informed him perpetually that if he felt anything, other than what disturbed him personally at first hand, he would suffer unnecessarily, and perhaps be encouraging such public action as might diminish his comfort. But he was no alarmist, and, on the whole, felt pretty sure that while he was there, living in Kent, with his plain views, there was no chance of anything being done that would cause him any serious inconvenience.

On the woman's question generally he had long made his position plain. He would move when the majority moved, and not before. And he expected all plain men (and women—if there were any, which he sometimes doubted) to act in the same way. In this policy he felt instinctively, rather than consciously, that there was no risk. No one—at least, no one that mattered, no plain, solid person—would move until he did, and he would not, of course, move until they did; in this way there was a perfectly plain position. And it was an extraordinary gratification to him to feel, from the tone of politicians, the pulpit, and the press, that he had the country with him. He often said to his wife: "One thing's plain to me; we shall never have the suffrage till the country wants it." But he rarely discussed the question with other women, having observed that many of them could not keep their tempers when he gave them his plain view of the matter.

He was sometimes at a loss to think what on earth they would do without him on juries, of which he was usually elected foreman. And he never failed to listen with pleasure to the words that never failed to be spoken to him: "As plain men, gentlemen, you will at once see how improbable in every particular is the argument of my friend." That he was valued in precisely the same way by both sides and ultimately by the judge filled him sometimes with a modest feeling that only a plain man was of any value whatever, certainly that he was the only kind of man who had any sort of judgment.

He often wondered what the country would do without him; into what abysmal trouble she would get in her politics, her art, her law, and her religion. It seemed to him that he alone stood between her and manifold destructions. How many times had he not seen her reeling in her cups and sophistries, and beckoning to him to save her! And had he ever failed her, with his simple philosophy of a plain man: "Follow me, and the rest will follow itself"? Never! As witness the veneration in which he saw that he was held every time he opened a paper, attended the performance of a play, heard a sermon, or listened to a speech. Some day he meant to sit for his portrait, believing that this was due from him to posterity; and now and then he would look into the glass to fortify his resolution. What he saw there always gave him secret pleasure. Here was a face that he knew he could trust, and even in a way admire. Nothing brilliant, showy, eccentric, soulful; nothing rugged, devotional, profound, or fiery; not even anything proud, or stubborn; no surplus of kindliness, sympathy, or aspiration; but just simple, solid lines, a fresh colour, and sensible, rather prominent eyes—just the face that he would have expected and desired, the face of a plain man.

IV.—The Superlative

Though he had not yet arrived, he had personally no doubt about the matter. It was merely a question of time. Not that for one moment he approved of "arriving" as a general principle. Indeed, there was no one whom he held in greater contempt than a man who had arrived. It was to him the high-water mark of imbecility, commercialism, and complacency. For what did it mean save that this individual had pleased a sufficient number of other imbeciles, hucksterers, and fat-heads, to have secured for himself a reputation? These pundits, these mandarins, these so-called "masters"—they were an offence to his common sense. He had passed them by, with all their musty and sham-Abraham achievements. That fine flair of his had found them out. Their mere existence was a scandal. Now and again one died; and his just anger would wane a little before the touch of the Great Remover. No longer did that pundit seem quite so objectionable now that he no longer cumbered the ground. It might even, perhaps, be admitted that there had been something coming out of that one; and, as the years rolled on, this something would roll on too, till it became quite a big thing; and he would compare those miserable pundits who still lived with the one who had so fortunately died, to their great disadvantage. There were, in truth, very few living beings that he could stand. Somehow they were not—no, they really *were not*. The great—as they were called forsooth—artists, writers, politicians—what were they? He would smile down one side of his long nose. It was enough. Forthwith those reputations ceased to breathe—for him. Their theories, too, of art, reform, what-not—how puerile! How utterly and hopelessly old-fashioned, how worthy of all the destruction that his pen and tongue could lavish on them!

For, to save his country's art, his country's literature and politics—that was, he well knew, his mission. And he periodically founded, or joined, the staff of papers that were going to do this trick. They always lasted several months, some several years, before breathing the last impatient sigh of genius. And while they lived, with what wonderful clean brooms they swept! Perched above all that miasma known as human nature, they beat the air, sweeping it and sweeping it, till suddenly there was no air left. And that theory, that real vision of art and existence, which they were going to put in place of all this muck, how near—how unimaginably near—they brought it to reality! Just another month, another year, another good sweeping, would have done it! And on that final ride of the broomstick, he—he would have arrived! At last some one would have been there with a real philosophy, a truly creative mind; some one whose poems and paintings, music, novels, plays, and measures of reform would at last have borne inspection! And he would go out from the office of that great paper so untimely wrecked, and, conspiring with himself, would found another.

This one should follow principles that could not fail. For, first, it should tolerate nothing—nothing at all. That was the mistake they had made last time. They had tolerated some reputations. No more of that; no—more! The imbeciles, the shallow frauds, let them be carted once for all. And with them let there be cremated the whole structure of society, all its worn-out formulas of art, religion, sociology. In place of them he would not this time be content to put nothing. No; it was the moment to elucidate and develop that secret rhyme and pulsation in the heart of the future hitherto undisclosed to any but himself. And all the time there should be flames going up out of that paper—the pale-red, the lovely flames of genius. Yes, the emanation should be wonderful. And, collecting his tattered mantle round his middle so small, he would start his race again.

For three numbers he would lay about him and outline religiously what was going to come. In the fourth number he would be compelled to concentrate himself on a final destruction of all those defences and spiteful counter-attacks which wounded vanity had wrung from the pundits, those apostles of the past; this final destruction absorbed his energies during the fifth, sixth, seventh, and eighth numbers. In the ninth he would say positively that he was now ready to justify the constructive prophecies of his first issues. In the tenth he would explain that, unless a blighted public supported an heroic effort better, genius would be withheld from them. In the eleventh number he would lay about him as he had never done, and in the twelfth give up the ghost.

In connection with him one had always to remember that he was not one of those complacent folk whose complacency stops short somewhere; his was a nobler kind, ever trying to climb into that heaven which he alone was going to reach some day. He had a touch of the divine discontent even with himself; and it was only in comparison with the rest of the world that he felt he was superlative.

It was a consolation to him that Nietzsche was dead, so that out of a full heart and empty conscience he could bang upon the abandoned drum of a man whom he scarcely hesitated to term great. And yet, what—as he often said—could be more dismally asinine than to see some of these live stucco moderns pretending to be supermen? Save this Nietzsche he admitted perhaps no philosopher into his own class, and was most down on Aristotle, and that one who had founded the religion of his country.

Of statesmen he held a low opinion—what were they, after all, but politicians? There was not one in the whole range of history who could take a view like an angel of the dawn surveying creation; not one who could soar above a contemptible adaptation of human means to human ends.

His poet was Blake. His playwright Strindberg, a man of distinct promise—fortunately dead. Of novelists he accepted Dostoievsky. Who else was there? Who else that had gone outside the range of normal, stupid, rational humanity, and shown the marvellous qualities of the human creature drunk or dreaming? Who else who had so arranged his scenery that from beginning to end one need never witness the dull shapes and colours of human life quite unracked by nightmare? It was in nightmare only that the human spirit revealed its possibilities.

In truth, he had a great respect for nightmare, even in its milder forms, the respect of one who felt that it was the only thing which an ordinary sane man could not achieve in his waking moments. He so hated the ordinary sane man, with his extraordinary lack of appreciative faculty.

In his artistic tastes he was paulo-post-futurist, and the painter he had elected to admire was one that no one had yet heard of. He meant, however, that they should hear of him when the moment came. With the arrival of that one would begin a new era of art, for which in the past there would be no parallel, save possibly one Chinese period long before that of which the pundits—poor devils—so blatantly bleated.

He was a connoisseur of music, and nothing gave him greater pain than a tune. Of all the ancients he recognised Bach alone, and only in his fugues. Wagner was considerable in places. Strauss and Debussy, well—yes, but now *vieux jeu*. There was an Esquimaux. His name? No, let them wait! That fellow was something. Let them mark his words, and wait!

It was for this kind of enlightenment of the world that he most ardently desired his own arrival, without which he sometimes thought he could no longer bear things as they were, no longer go on watching his chariot unhitched to a star, trailing the mud of this musty, muddled world, whose ethics even, those paltry wrappings of the human soul, were uncongenial to him.

Talking of ethics, there was one thing especially that he absolutely could not bear—that second-hand creature, a gentleman; the notion that his own superlative self should be compelled by some mouldy and incomprehensible tradition to respect the feelings or see the point of view of others—this was indeed the limit. No, no! To bound upon the heads and limbs the prejudices and convictions of those he came in contact with, especially in print, that was a holy duty. And, though conscientious to a degree, there was certainly no one of all his duties that he performed so conscientiously as this. No amenities defiled his tongue or pen, nor did he ever shrink from personalities—his spiritual honesty was terrific. But he never thrust or cut where it was not deserved; practically the whole world was open to his scorn, as he well knew, and he never needed to go out of his way to find victims for it. Indeed, he made no cult at all of eccentricity—that was for smaller creatures. His dress, for instance, was of the soberest, save that now and then he would wear a purple shirt, grey boots, or a yellow-ochre tie. His life and habits, lost in the future, were, on the whole, abstemious. He had no children, but set great store by them, and fully meant when he had time to have quite a number, for this was, he knew, his duty to a world breeding from mortal men. Whether they would arrive before he did was a question, since, until then, his creative attention could hardly be sufficiently disengaged.

At times he scarcely knew himself, so absorbed was he; but you knew him because he breathed rather hard, as became a man lost in creation. In the higher flights of his genius he paused for nothing, not even for pen and paper; he touched the clouds, indeed—and, like the clouds, height piled on vaporous height, his images and conceptions hung wreathed, immortal, evanescent as the very air. It was an annoyance to him afterward to find that he had neglected to pin them to earth. Still, with his intolerance of all except divinity, and his complete faith that he must in time achieve it, he was perhaps the most interesting person to be found in the purlieus of—wherever it might be.

V.—The Preceptor

He had a philosophy as yet untouched. His stars were the old stars, his faith the old faith; nor would he recognise that there was any other, for not to recognise any point of view except his own was no doubt the very essence of his faith. Wisdom! There was surely none save the flinging of the door to, standing with your back against the door, and telling people what was behind it. For, though he also could not know what was behind, he thought it low to say so. An "atheist," as he termed certain persons, was to him beneath contempt, an "agnostic," as he termed certain others, a poor and foolish creature. As for a rationalist, positivist, pragmatist or any other "ist"—well, that was just what they were. He made no secret of the fact that he simply could not understand people like that. It was true. "What can they do—save deny?" he would say. "What do they contribute to the morals and the elevation of the world? What do they put in the place of what they take away? What have they got, to make up for what is behind that door? Where are their symbols? How shall they move and lead the people? No," he said, "a little child shall lead the people, and I am the little child! For I can spin them a tale such as children love, of what is behind the door." Such was the temper of his mind that he never flinched from believing true what he thought would benefit himself and others. For example, he held a crown of ultimate advantage to be necessary to induce pure and stable living. If one could not say: "Listen, children! there it is, behind the door! Look at it, shining, golden—yours! Not now, but when you die, if you are good. Be good, therefore! For if you are not good—no crown!" If one could not say that—what could one say? What inducement hold out? And warmly he would describe the crown! There was nothing he detested more than commercialism. And to any one who ventured to suggest that there was something rather commercial about the idea of that crown, he would retort with asperity. A mere creed that good must be done, so to speak, just out of a present love of dignity and beauty—as a man, seeing something he admired, might work to reproduce it, knowing that he would never achieve it perfectly, but going on until he dropped, out of sheer love of going on—he thought vague, futile, devoid of glamour and contrary to human nature, for he always judged people by himself, and felt that no one could like to go on unless they knew that they would get something if they did. To promise victory, therefore, was most important. Forlorn hopes, setting your teeth, back to the wall, and such like, was bleak and wintry doctrine, without inspiration in it, because it led to nothing—so far as he could see. Those others, who, not presuming to believe in anything, went on, because—as they said—to give up would be to lose their honour, seemed to him poor lost creatures who had denied faith; and faith was, as has been said, the mainspring of his philosophy.

Once, indeed, in the unguarded moment of a heated argument, he had confessed that some day men might not require to use the symbols of religion which they used now. It was at once pointed out to him that, if he thought that, he could not believe these symbols to be true for all time; and if they were not true for all time, why did he say they were? He was dreadfully upset. Deferring answer, however, for the moment, he was soon able to retort that the symbols were true—er—mystically. If a man—and this was the point—did not stand by *these* symbols, by which could he stand? Tell him that! Symbols were necessary. But what symbols were there in a mere good will; a mere vague following of one's own dignity and honour, out of a formless love of life? How put up a religion of such amorphous and unrewarded chivalry and devotion, how put up a blind love of mystery, in place of a religion of definite crowns and punishments, how substitute a worship of mere abstract goodness, or beauty, for worship of what could be called by Christian names? Human nature being what it was—it would not do, it absolutely would not do. Though he was fond of the words "mystery," "mystical," he had emphatically no use for them when they were vaguely used by people to express their perpetual (and quite unmoral) reverence for the feeling that they would never find out the secret of their own existence, never even understand the nature of the universe or God. Fancy! Mystery of that kind seemed to him pagan, almost nature-worship, having no finality. And if confronted by some one who said that a Mystery, *if* it could be understood, would naturally not be a mystery, he would raise his eyebrows. It was that kind of loose, specious, sentimental talk that did so much harm, and drew people away from right understanding of that Great Mystery which, if it was *not* understood and properly explained, was, for all practical purposes, not a great mystery at all. No, it had all been gone into long ago, and he stood by the explanations and intended that every one else should, for in that way alone men were saved; and, though he well knew (for he was no Jesuit) that the end did not justify the means, yet in a matter of such all-importance one stopped to consider neither means nor ends—one just saved people. And as for truth—the question of that did not arise, if one believed. What one believed, what one was told to believe, *was* the truth; and it was no good telling him that the whole range of a man's feeling and reasoning powers must be exercised to ascertain truth, and that, when ascertained, it would only be relative truth, and the best available to that particular man. Nothing short of the absolute truth would *he* put up with, and that guaranteed fixed and immovable, or it was no good for his purpose. To any one who threw out doubts here and doubts there, and even worse than doubts, he had long formed the habit of saying simply, with a smile that he tried hard to make indulgent: "Of course, if you believe *that!*"

But he very seldom had to argue on these matters, because people, looking at his face with its upright bone-formation, rather bushy eyebrows, and eyes with a good deal of light in them, felt that it would be simpler not. He seemed to them to know his own mind almost too well. Joined to this potent faculty of implanting in men a childlike trustfulness in what he told them was behind the door, he had a still more potent faculty of knowing exactly what was good for them in everyday life. The secret of this power was simple. He did not recognise the existence of what moderns and so-called "artists" dubbed "temperament." All talk of that sort was bosh, and generally immoral bosh; for all moral purposes people really had but one temperament, and that was, of course, just like his own. And no one knew better than he what was good for it. He was perfectly willing to recognise the principle of individual treatment for individual cases; but it did not do, in practice, he was convinced, to vary. This instinctive wisdom made him invaluable in all those departments of life where discipline and the dispensation of an even justice were important. To adapt men to the moral law was—he thought—

perhaps the first duty of a preceptor, especially in days when there was perceptible a distinct but regrettable tendency to try and adapt the moral law to the needs—as they were glibly called—of men. There was, perhaps, in him something of the pedagogue, and when he met a person who disagreed with him his eyes would shift a bit to the right and a bit to the left, then become firmly fixed upon that person from under brows rather drawn down; and his hand, large and strong, would move fingers, as if more and more tightly grasping a cane, birch, or other wholesome instrument. He loved his fellow-creatures so that he could not bear to see them going to destruction for want of a timely flogging to salvation.

He was one of those who seldom felt the need for personal experience of a phase of life, or line of conduct, before giving judgment on it; indeed, he gravely distrusted personal experience. He had opposed, for instance all relief for the unhappily married long before he left the single state; and, when he did leave it, would not admit for a moment that his own happiness was at all responsible for the petrifaction of his view that no relief was necessary. Hard cases made bad law! But he did not require to base his opinion upon that. He said simply that he had been told there was to be no relief—it was enough.

The saying "To understand all is to forgive all!" left him cold. It was, as he well knew, quite impossible to identify himself with such conditions as produced poverty, disease and crime, even if he wished to do so (which he sometimes doubted). He knew better, therefore, than to waste his time attempting the impossible; and he pinned his faith to an instinctive knowledge of how to deal with all such social ills: A contented spirit for poverty; for disease isolation; and for crime such punishment as would at once deter others, reform the criminal, and convince every one that law must be avenged and the social conscience appeased. On this point of revenge he was emphatic. No vulgar personal feeling of vindictiveness, of course, but a strong state feeling of "an eye for an eye." It was the only taint of socialism that he permitted himself. Loose thinkers, he knew, dared to say that a desire for retribution or revenge was a purely human or individual feeling like hate, love, and jealousy; and that to talk of satisfying such a feeling in the collected bosom of the state was either to talk nonsense—how could a state have a bosom?—or to cause the bosoms of the human individuals who administered the justice of the state to feel that each of them was itself that stately bosom, and entitled to be revengeful. "Oh, no!" he would answer to such loose-thinking persons; "judges, of course, give expression not to what they feel themselves but to what they imagine the state feels." He himself, for example, was perfectly able to imagine which crimes were those that inspired in the bosom of the state a particular abhorrence, a particular desire to be avenged; now it was blackmail, now assaults upon children, or living on the earnings of immoral women; he was certain that the state regarded all these with peculiar detestation, for he had, and quite rightly, a particular detestation of them himself; and if he were a judge, he would never for a moment hesitate to visit on the perpetrators of such vile crimes the utmost vengeance of the law. He was no loose thinker. In these times, bedridden with loose thinking and sickly sentiment, he often felt terribly the value of his own philosophy, and was afraid that it was in danger. But not many other people held that view, discerning his finger still very large in every pie—so much so that there often seemed less pie than finger.

It would have shocked him much to realise that he could be considered a fit subject for a study of extravagance; fortunately, he had not the power of seeing himself as others saw him, nor was there any danger that he ever would.

VI.—The Artist

He had long known, of course, that to say the word "bourgeois" with contempt was a little bit old-fashioned, and he did his utmost not to; yet was there a still small voice within him that would whisper: "Those people—I want to and I do treat them as my equals. I have even gone so far of late years as to dress like them, to play their games, to eat regularly, to drink little, to love decorously, with many other bourgeois virtues, but in spite of all I remain where I was, an inhabitant of another—" and, just as he thought the whispering voice was going to die away, it would add hurriedly—"and a better world."

It worried him; and he would diligently examine the premises of that small secret conclusion, hoping to find a flaw in the justness of his conviction that he was superior. But he never did; and for a long time he could not discover why.

Often the conduct of the "bourgeois" would strike him as almost superfluously good. They were brave, much braver than he was conscious of being; clean-thinking, oh, far more clean-thinking than a man like himself, necessarily given to visions of all kinds; they were straightforward, almost ridiculously so, as it seemed to one who saw the inside-out of everything almost before he saw the outside-out; they were simple, as touchingly simple as those little children, to whom Scriptures and post-impressionism had combined to award the crown of wisdom; they were kind and self-denying in a way that often made him feel quite desperately his own selfishness—and yet—they were inferior. It was simply maddening that he could never rid himself of that impression.

It was one November afternoon, while talking with another artist, that the simple reason struck him with extraordinary force and clarity: *He could make them, and they could not make him!*

It was clearly this which caused him to feel so much like God when they were about. Glad enough, as any man might be, of that discovery, it did not set his mind at rest. He felt that he ought rather to be humbled than elated. And he went to work at once to be so, saying to himself: "I am just, perhaps, a little nearer to the Creative Purpose than the rest of the world—a mere accident, nothing to be proud of; I can't help it, nothing to make a fuss about, though people will!" For it did seem to him sometimes that the whole world was in conspiracy to make him feel superior—as if there were any need! He would have felt much more comfortable if that world had despised him, as it used to in the old days, for then the fire of his conviction could with so much better grace have flared to heaven; there would have been something fine about a superiority leading its own forlorn hope. But this trailing behind the drums and trumpets of a press and public so easily taken in he felt to be both flat and a little degrading. True, he had his moments, as when his eyes would light on sentences like this (penned generally by clergymen): "All this talk of art is idle; what really matters is morals." Then, indeed, his spirit would flame, and after gazing at "is morals" with flashing eye and curling lip, and wondering whether it ought to have been "are morals," he would say to whomsoever might happen to be there: "These bourgeois! What do they know? What can they see?" and, without waiting for an answer, would reply: "Nothing! Nothing! Less than nothing!" and mean it. It was at moments such as these that he realised how he not only despised, but almost hated, those dense and cocky Philistines who could not see his obvious superiority. He felt that he did not lightly call them by such names, because they really *were* dense and cocky, and no more able to see things from his point of view than they were to jump over the moon. These fellows could see nothing except from their own confounded view-point! They were so stodgy too; and he gravely distrusted anything static. Flux, flux, and once more flux! He knew by intuition that an artist alone had the capacity for concreting the tides of life in forms that were not deleterious to anybody. For rules and canons he recognised the necessity with his head (including his tongue), but never with his heart; except, of course, the rules and canons of art. He worshipped these; and when anybody like Tolstoi came along and said, "Blow art!" or words to that effect, he hummed like bees caught on a gust of wind. What did it matter whether you had anything to express, so long as you expressed it? That only was "pure æsthetics," as he often said. To place before the public eye something so exquisitely purged of thick and muddy actuality that it might be as perfectly without direct appeal today as it would be two thousand years hence—this was an ambition to which in truth he nearly always attained; this only was great art. He would assert with his last breath—which was rather short, for he suffered from indigestion—that one must never concrete anything in terms of ordinary nature. No! one must devise pictures of life that would be equally unfamiliar to men in A.D. 2520 as they had been in A.D. 1920; and when an inconsiderate person drew his attention to the fact that to the spectator in 2520 the most naturalistic pictures of the life of 1920 would seem quite convincingly fantastic, so that there was no need for him to go out of his way to devise fantasy—he would stare. For he was emphatically not one of those who did not care a button what the form was so long as the spirit of the artist shone clear and potent through the pictures he drew. No, no; he either demanded the poetical, the thing that got off the ground, with the wind in its hair (and he himself would make the wind, rather perfumed); or—if not the poetical—something observed with extreme fidelity and without the smallest touch of that true danger to art, the temperamental point of view. "No!" he would say; "it's our business to put it down just as it is, to see it, not to feel it. In feeling damnation lies." And nothing gave him greater uneasiness than to find the emotions of anger, scorn, love, reverence, or pity surging within him as he worked, for he knew that they would, if he did not at once master them, spoil a certain splendid vacuity that he demanded of all art. In painting, Raphael, Tintoretto, and Holbein pleased him greatly; in fiction, "Salammbô" was his model, for, as he very justly said, you could supply to it what soul you liked—there being no inconvenient soul already in possession.

As can be well imagined, his conviction of being, in a small way, God, permeated an outlook that was passionless, and impartial to a degree—except perhaps toward the bourgeoisie, with their tiring morals and peculiar habits. If he had a weakness, it was his paramount desire to suppress in himself any symptoms of temperament, except just that temperament of having no temperament, which seemed to him the only one permissible to an artist, who, as he said, was nothing if not simply either a recorder or a weaver of beautiful lines in the air.

Record and design, statement and decoration—these, in combination, constituted creation! It was to him a certain source of pleasure that he had discovered this. Not that he was, of course, neglectful of sensations, but he was perfectly careful not to *feel* them—in order that he might be able to record them, or use them for his weaving in a purely æsthetic manner. The moment they impinged on his spirit, and sent the blood to his head, he reined in, and began tracing lines in the air, a practice that never failed him.

It was his deliberate opinion that a work of art quite as great as the "Bacchus and Ariadne" could be made out of a kettle singing on a hob. You had merely to record it with beautiful lines and colour; and what—in parenthesis—could lend itself more readily to beautiful treatment of lines woven in the air than steam rising from a spout? It was a subject, too, which in its very essence almost precluded temperamental treatment, so that this abiding temptation was removed from the creator. It could be transferred to canvas with a sort of immortal blandness—black, singing, beautiful. All that cant, such as, "The greater the artist's spirit, the greater the subject he will treat, and the greater achievement attain, technique being equal," was to him beneath contempt. The spirit did not matter, because one must not intrude it; and, since one must not intrude it, the more unpretentious the subject, the less temptation one had to diverge from impersonality, that first principle of art. Oranges on a dish afforded probably the finest subject one could meet with; unless one chanced to dislike oranges. As for what people called "criticism of life," he maintained that such was only permissible when the criticism was so sunk into the very fibre of a work as to be imperceptible to the most searching eye. When this was achieved he thought it extremely valuable. Anything else was simply the work of the moralist, of the man who took sides and used his powers of expression to embody a temperamental and therefore an obviously one-sided view of his subject; and, however high those powers of expression might be, he could not admit that this was in any sense real art. He could never forgive Leonardo da Vinci, because, he said, "the fellow was always trying to put the scientific side of himself into his confounded paintings, and not just content to render faithfully in terms of decoration"; nor could he ever condone Euripides for letting his philosophy tincture his plays. And, if it were advanced that the former was the greatest painter and the latter the greatest dramatist the world had ever seen, he would say: "That may be, but they weren't artists, of course."

He was fond of the words "of course"; they gave the impression that he could not be startled, as was right and proper for a man occupying his post, a little nearer to the Creative Purpose than those others. As mark of that position, he always permitted himself just one eccentricity, changing it every year, his mind being subtle—not like those of certain politicians or millionaires, content to wear orchids or drive zebras all their lives. Anon it would be a little pointed beard and no hair to speak of; next year, no beard, and wings; the year after, a pair of pince-nez with alabaster rims, very cunning; once more anon, a little pointed beard. In these ways he singled himself out just enough, no more; for he was no *poseur*, believing in his own place in the scheme of things too deeply.

His views on matters of the day varied, of course, with the views of those he talked to, since it was his privilege always to see either the other side or something so much more subtle on the same side as made that side the other.

But all topical thought and emotion was beside the point for one who lived in his work; who lived to receive impressions and render them again so faithfully that you could not tell he had ever received them. His was—as he sometimes felt—a rare and precious personality.

VII.—The Housewife

Though frugal by temperament, and instinctively aware that her sterling nature was the bank in which the national wealth was surely deposited, she was of benevolent disposition; and when, as occasionally happened, a man in the street sold her one of those jumping toys for her children, she would look at him and say:

"How much? You don't look well!" and he would answer: "Tuppence, lidy. Truth is, lidy, I've gone 'ungry this lawst week." Searching his face shrewdly, she would reply: "That's bad—a sin against the body. Here's threepence. Give me a ha'penny. You don't look well." And, taking the ha'penny, she would leave the man inarticulate.

Food appealed to her, not only in relation to herself, but to others. Often to some friend she would speak a little bitterly, a little mournfully, about her husband. "Yes, I quite like my 'hubby' to go out sometimes where he can talk about art, and war, and things that women can't. He takes no interest in his food." And she would add, brooding: "What he'd do if I didn't study him, I really don't know." She often felt with pain that he was very thin. She studied him incessantly—that is, in due proportion to their children, their position in society, their Christianity, and herself. If he was her "hubby," she was his "hub"—the housewife, that central pivot of society, that national pivot, which never could or would be out of gear. Devoid of conceit, it seldom occurred to her to examine her own supremacy, quietly content to be "integer vitæ, scelerisque pura"—just the one person against whom nobody could say anything. Subconsciously, no doubt, she *must* have valued her worth and reputation, or she would never have felt such salutary gusts of irritation and contempt toward persons who had none. Like cows when a dog comes into a field, she would herd together whenever she saw a woman with what she suspected was a past, then advance upon her, horns down. If the offending creature did not speedily vacate the field, she would, if possible, trample her to death. When, by any chance, the female dog proved too swift and lively, she would remain sullenly turning and turning her horns in the direction of its vagaries. Well she knew that, if she once raised those horns and let the beast pass, her whole herd would suffer. There was something almost magnificent about her virtue, based, as it was, entirely on self-preservation, and her remarkable power of rejecting all premises except those familiar to herself. This gave it a fibre and substance hard as concrete. Here, indeed, was something one could build on; here, indeed, was the strait thing. Her husband would sometimes say to her: "My dear, we don't know what the poor woman's circumstances were, we really don't, you know. I think we should try to put ourselves in her place." And she would fix his eye, and say: "James, it's no good. I can't imagine myself in that woman's place, and I won't. Do you think that *I* would ever leave *you*?" And, watching till he shook his head, she would go on: "Of course not. No. Nor let you leave me." And, pausing a second, to see if he blinked, because men were rather like that (even those who had the best of wives), she would go on: "She deserves all she gets. I have no personal feeling, but, if once decent women begin to get soft about this sort of thing, then good-bye to family life and Christianity, and everything. I'm not hard, but there are things I feel strongly about, and this is one of them." And secretly she would think: "That's why he keeps so thin—always letting himself doubt, and sympathise, where one has no right to. Men!" Next time she passed the woman, she would cut her deader than the last time, and, seeing her smile, would feel a sort of divine fury. More than once this had led her into courts of law on charges of libel and slander. But, knowing how impregnable was her position, she almost welcomed that opportunity. For it was ever transparent to judge and jury from the first that she was that crown of pearls, a virtuous woman, and so she was never cast in damages.

On one such occasion her husband had been so ill-advised as to remark: "My dear, I have my doubts whether our duty does not stop at seeing to ourselves, without throwing stones at others."

"Robert," she had answered, "if you think that, just because there's a chance that you may have to pay damages, I'm going to hold my tongue when vice flaunts itself, you make a mistake. I always put your judgment above mine, but this is not a matter of judgment—it is a matter of Christian and womanly conduct. I can't admit even your right to dictate."

She hated that expression, "The grey mare is the better horse"; it was vulgar, and she would never recognise its truth in her own case—for a wife's duty was to submit herself to her husband, as she had already said. After this little incident she took the trouble to go and open her New Testament and look up the story of a certain woman. There was not a word in it about women not throwing stones; the discouragement referred entirely to men. Exactly! No one knew better than she the difference between men and women in the matter of moral conduct. Probably there *were* no men without that kind of sin, but there were plenty of women, and, without either false or true pride, she felt that she was one of them. And there the matter rested.

Her views on political and social questions—on the whole, very simple—were to be summed up in the words, "That *man*—!" and, so far as it lay in her power, she saw to it that her daughters should not have any views at all. She found this, however, an increasingly hard task, and on one occasion was almost terrified to find her first and second girls abusing "that man—," not for going too fast, but for not going fast enough. She spoke to William about it, but found him hopeless, as usual, where his daughters were concerned. It was her principle to rule them with good, motherly sense, as became a woman in whose hands the family life of her country centred; and it was satisfactory on the whole to find that they obeyed her whenever they wished to. On this occasion, however, she spoke to them severely: "The place of woman," she said, "is in the home." "The whole home—and nothing but the home." "Ella! The place of women is by the side of man; counselling, supporting, ruling, but never competing with him. The place of woman is in the shop, the kitchen, and—" "The—bed!" "*Ella!*" "In the soup!" "Beatrice! I wish—I do wish you girls would be more respectful. The place of woman is in the home. Yes, I've said that before, but I shall say it again, and don't you forget it! The place of woman is—the most important thing in national life. If you want to realise that, just think of your own mother; and—" "Our own father." "Ella! The place of woman is in the—!" She left the room, feeling that, for the moment, she had said enough.

In disposition sociable, and no niggard of her company, there was one thing she liked to work at alone—her shopping, an art which she had long reduced to a science. The principles she laid down are worth remembering: Never grudge your time to save a ha'penny. Never buy anything until you have turned it well over, recollecting that the rest of you will have turned it over too. Never let your feelings of pity interfere with your sense of justice, but bear in mind that the girls who sell to you are paid for doing it; if you can afford the time to keep them on their legs, they can afford the time to let you. Never read pamphlets, for you don't know what may be in them about furs, feathers, and forms of food. Never buy more than your husband can afford to pay for; but, on the whole, buy as much. Never let any seller see that you think you have bought a bargain, but buy one if you can; you will find it pleasant afterward to talk of your prowess. Shove, shove, and shove again!

In the perfect application of these principles, she had found, after long experience, that there was absolutely no one to touch her.

In regard to meat, she had sometimes thought she would like to give it up, because she had read in her paper that being killed hurt the poor animals; but she had never gone beyond thought, because it was very difficult to do that. Henry was thin, and distinctly pale; the girls were growing girls; Sunday would hardly seem Sunday without; besides, it did not do to believe what one read in the paper, and it would hurt her butcher's feelings—she was sure of that. Christmas, too, stood in the way. It was one's duty to be cheerful at that season, and Christmas would seem so strange without the cheery butchers' shops and their appropriate holocaust. She had once read some pages of a disgraceful book that seemed going out of its way all the time to prove that *she* was just an animal—a dreadful book, not at all nice! And if she would eat those creatures if they were really her brother animals, and not just sent by God to feed her. No; at Christmas she felt especially grateful to the good God for his abundance, for all the good things he gave her to eat. For all these reasons she swallowed her scruples religiously. But it was very different in regard to dairy produce; for here there was, she knew, a real danger—not, indeed, to the animals, but to her family and herself. She was for once really proud of the thoroughness with which she dealt with that important nourishment—milk. None came into her house except in sealed bottles, with the name of the cow, spiritually speaking, on the outside. Some wag had suggested, in her hearing, that hens should be compelled to initial their eggs when they were delivered, as well as to put the dates on them. This she had thought ribald; one could go too far.

She was, before all things, an altruist; and in nothing more so than in her relations with her servants. If they did not do their duty, they went. It was the only way, she had found, to really benefit them. Country girls and town girls, they passed from her in a stream, having learned, once for all, the standard that was expected from them. She christened and educated more servants, perhaps, than any one in the kingdom. The Marthas went first, being invariably dirty; the Marys and Susans lasted, on an average, perhaps four months, and then left for many reasons. Cook seldom hurried off before her year was over, because it was so difficult to get her before she came, and to replace her after she was gone; but when she did go it was in a gale of wind. The "day out" was, perhaps, the most fruitful source of disillusionment—girls of that class, no matter how much they protested their innocence, seemed utterly unable to keep away from man's society. It was only once a fortnight that she required them to exercise their self-control and self-respect in that regard, for on the other thirteen days she took care that they had no chance, suffering no male footstep in her basement. And yet—would you believe it?—on those fourteenth days, she was never able to be easy in her mind. But, however kindly and considerate she might be in her dealings with those of lowly station, she found ever the same ingratitude, the same incapacity, or, as she had reluctantly been forced to believe, the same deliberate unwillingness to grasp her point of view. It was as if they were always rudely saying to themselves: "What do you know of us? We wish you'd leave us alone!" The idea! As if she could, or would! As if it were not an almost sacred charge on her in her station, with the responsibilities that attached to it, to look after her poorer neighbours and see that they acted properly in their own interests. The drink, the immorality, the waste amongst the poor was notorious, and anything she could do to lessen it she always did, dismissing servants for the least slip, and never failing to point a moral. All that new-fangled talk about the rich getting off the backs of the poor, about the law not being the same for both, about how easy it was to be moral and clean on two thousand a year, she put aside as silly. It was just the sort of thing that discontented people would say. In this view she was supported daily by her newspaper and herself, wherever she might be. No, no! If the well-to-do did not look after and control the poor, no one would, which was just what they would like. They were, in her estimation, incurable; but, so far as lay in her power, she would cure them, however painful it might be.

A religious woman, she rarely missed the morning, and seldom went to evening, service, feeling that in daylight she could best set an example to her neighbours.

God knew her views on art, for she was not prodigal of them—her most remarkable pronouncement being delivered on hearing of the disappearance of the "Monna Lisa": "Oh, that dreadful woman! I remember her picture perfectly. Well, I'm glad she's gone. I thought she would some day." When asked why, she would only answer: "She gave me the creeps."

She read such novels as the library sent, to save her daughters from reading a second time those which did not seem to her suitable, and promptly sent them back. In this way she preserved purity in her home. As to purity outside the home, she made a point of never drawing Frederick's attention to female beauty; not that she felt she had any real reason to be alarmed, for she was a fine woman; but because men were so funny.

There were no things in life of which she would have so entirely disapproved, if she had known about them, as Greek ideals, for she profoundly distrusted any display of the bare limb, and fully realised that, whatever beauty may have meant to the Greeks, to her and George it meant something very different. To her, indeed, Nature was a "hussy," to be tied to the wheels of that chariot which she was going to keep as soon as motorcars were just a little cheaper and really reliable.

It was often said that she was a vanishing type, but she knew better. Pedantic fools murmured that Ibsen had destroyed her, but she had not yet heard of him. Literary folk and artists, socialists and society people, might talk of types, and liberty, of brotherhood, and new ideas, and sneer at Mrs. Grundy. With what unmoved solidity she dwelt among them! They were but as gadflies, buzzing and darting on the fringes of her central bulk. To those flights, to that stinging she paid less attention than if she had been cased in leather. In the words of her favourite Tennyson: "They may come, and they may go, but—whatever you may think—I go on forever!"

VIII.—The Latest Thing

There was in her blood that which bade her hasten, lest there should be something still new to her when she died. Death! She was continually haunted by the fear lest that itself might be new. And she would say: "Do you know what it feels like to be dead? I do." If she had not known this, she felt that she would not have lived her life to the full. And one must live one's life to the full. Indeed, yes! One must experience everything. In her relations with men, for instance, there was nothing, so far as she could see, to prevent her from being a good wife, good mother, good mistress, and good friend—to different men all at the same time, and even to more than one man of each kind, if necessary. One had merely to be oneself, a full nature, giving and taking generously. Greed was a low and contemptible attribute, especially in woman; a woman wanted nothing more than—everything, and the best of that. And it was intolerable if one could not have that little. Woman had always been kept down. Not to be kept down was still, on the whole, new. Yet sometimes, after she had not been kept down rather violently, she would feel: Oh, the weariness! I shall throw it all up, and live on a shilling a day, like a sweated worker—that, at all events, will be new! She even sometimes dreamed of retirement to convent life—the freshness of its old-world novelty appealed to her.

To such an idealist, the very colours of the rainbow did not suffice, nor all the breeds of birds there were; her life was piled high with cages. Here she had had them one by one, borrowed their songs, relieved them of their plumes; then, finding that they no longer had any, let them go; for to look at things without possessing them was intolerable, but to keep them when she had got them even more so.

She often wondered how people could get along at all whose natures were not so full as hers. Life, she thought, must be so dull for the poor creatures, only doing one thing at a time, and that time so long. What with her painting, and her music, her dancing, her flying, her motoring, her writing of novels and poems, her love-making, maternal cares, entertaining, friendships, housekeeping, wifely duties, political and social interests, her gardening, talking, acting, her interest in Russian linen and the woman's movement; what with travelling in new countries, listening to new preachers, lunching new novelists, discovering new dancers, taking lessons in Spanish; what with new dishes for dinner, new religions, new dogs, new dresses, new duties to new neighbours, and newer charities—life was so full that the moment it stood still and was simply old "life," it seemed to be no life at all.

She could not bear the amateur; feeling within herself some sacred fire that made her "an artist" whatever she took up—or dropped. She had a particular dislike, too, of machine-made articles; for her, personality must be deep-woven into everything—look at flowers, how wonderful they were in that way, growing quietly to perfection, each in its corner, and inviting butterflies to sip their dew! She knew, for she had been told it so often, that she was the crown of creation—the latest thing in women, who were, of course, the latest thing in creatures. There had never, till quite recently, been a woman like her, so awfully interested in so many things, so likely to be interested in so many more. She had flung open all the doors of life, and was so continually going out and coming in, that life had some considerable difficulty in catching a glimpse of her at all. Just as the cinematograph was the future of the theatre, so was she the future of women, and in the words of the poet "prou' title." To sip at every flower before her wings closed; if necessary, to make new flowers to sip at. To smoke the whole box of cigarettes straight off, and in the last puff of smoke expire! And withal, no feverishness, only a certain reposeful and womanly febrility; a mere perpetual glancing from quick-sliding eyes, to see the next move, to catch the new movement—God bless it! And, mind you, a high sense of duty—perhaps a higher sense of duty than that of any woman who had gone before; a deep and intimate conviction that women had an immensity of leeway to make up, that their old, starved, stunted lives must be avenged, and that right soon. To enlarge the horizon— this was the sacred duty! No mere Boccaccian or Louis Quinze cult of plea- surable sensations; no crude, lolling, plutocratic dollery of a spoiled dame. No! the full, deep river of sensations nibbling each other's tails. Life was real, life was earnest, and time the essence of its contract.

To say that she had favourite books, plays, men, dogs, colours, was to do her but momentary justice. A deeper equity assigned her only one fa- vourite—the next; and, for the sake of that one favourite, no Catharine, no Semiramis or Messalina, could more swiftly dispose of all the others. With what avidity she sprang into its arms, drained its lips of kisses, looking hur- riedly the while for its successor; for Heaven alone—she felt—knew what would happen to her if she finished drinking before she caught sight of that next necessary one.

And yet, now and again, time played her false, and she got through too soon. It was then that she realised the sensation of death. After the first ter- rible inanition, those moments lived without "living" would begin to assume a sort of preciousness, to acquire holy sensations of their own. "I am dead," she would say to herself: "I really am dead; I lie motionless, hearing, feeling, smelling, seeing, thinking nothing. I lie impalpable—yes, that is the word— completely impalpable; above me I can see the vast blue blue, and all around me the vast brown brown—it is something like what I remember of Egypt. And there is a kind of singing in my ears, that are really not ears now, a grey, thin sound, like—ah!—Maeterlinck, and a very faint honey smell, like— er—Omar Khayyám. And I just move as a blade of grass moves in the wind. Yes, I am dead. It feels exactly like it." And a new exhilaration would seize her, for she felt that, in that sensation of death, she was living! At lunch, or it might be dinner, she would tell her newest man, already past the prime of her interest, exactly what it felt like to be dead. "It's not really disagreeable," she would say; "it has its own flavour. You know, like Turkish coffee, just a touch of india-rubber in it—I mean the coffee." And the poor man would sneeze, and answer: "Yes, I know a little what you mean; asphodels, too; you get it in Greece. My only difficulty is that, if you *are* dead, you know— you—er—are." She would not admit that; it sounded true, but the man was getting stupid—to be dead like that would be the end of novelty, which was, to her, unthinkable.

Once, in a new book, she came across a little tale of a man who "lived" in Persia, of all heavenly places, frantically pursuing sensation. Entering one day the courtyard of his house, he heard a sigh behind him, and, looking round, saw his own spirit, apparently in the act of breathing its last. The little thing, dry and pearly-white as a seed-pod of "honesty," was opening and shutting its mouth, for all the world like an oyster trying to breathe. "What is it?" he said; "you don't seem well." And his spirit answered: "All right, all right! Don't distress yourself—it's nothing! I've just been crowded out. That's all. Good-bye!" And, with a wheeze, the little thing went flat, fell onto the special blue tiles he had caused to be put down there, and lay still. He bent to pick it up, but it came off on his thumb in a smudge of grey-white powder.

This fancy was so new that it pleased her greatly, and she recommended the book to all her friends. The moral, of course, was purely Eastern, and had no applicability whatever to Western life, where, the more one did and expressed, the bigger and more healthy one's spirit grew—as witness what she always felt to be going on within herself. But next spring she changed the blue tiles of her Persian smoking-room, put in a birch-wood floor, and made it all Russian. This she did, however, merely because one new room a year was absolutely essential to her spirit.

In her perpetual journey toward an ever-widening horizon of woman's life, she was not so foolish as to prize danger for its own sake—that was by no means her idea of adventure. That she ran some risks it would be idle to deny, but only when she had discerned the substantial advantage of a new sensation to be had out of adventures, not at all because they were necessary to keep her soul alive. She was, she felt, a Greek in spirit, only more so perhaps, having in her also something of America and the West End.

How she came to be at all was only known to that age—whose daughter she undoubtedly was—an age which ran all the time, without any foolish notion where it was running to. There was no novelty in a destination, and no sensation to be had from sitting cross-legged in a tub of sunlight—not, at least, after you had done it once. *She* had been born to dance the moon down, to ragtime. The moon, the moon! Ah, yes! It was the one thing that had as yet eluded her avidity. That, and her own soul.

IX.—The Perfect One

When you had seen him you knew that there was really nothing to be said. Idealism, humanity, culture, philosophy, the religious and æsthetic senses—after all, where did all that lead? Not to him! What led to him was beef, and whisky, exercise, wine, strong cigars, and open air. What led to him was anything that ministered to the coatings of the stomach and the thickness of the skin. In seeing him, you also saw how progress, civilisation, and refinement simply meant attrition of those cuticles which made him what he was. And what was he? Well—perfect! Perfect for that high, that supreme purpose—the enjoyment of life as it was. And, aware of his perfection—oh, well aware!—with a certain blind astuteness that refused reflection on the subject—not caring what anybody said or thought, just enjoying himself, taking all that came his way, and making no bones about it; unconscious, indeed, that there were any to be made. He must have known by instinct that thought, feeling, sympathy only made a man chickeny, for he avoided them in an almost sacred way. To be "hard" was his ambition, and he moved through life hitting things, especially balls—whether they reposed on little inverted tubs of sand, or moved swiftly toward him, he almost always hit them, and told people how he did it afterward. He hit things, too, at a distance, through a tube, with a certain noise, and a pleasant swelling sensation under his fifth rib every time he saw them tumble, feeling that they had swollen still more under their fifth ribs and would not require to be hit again. He tried to hit things in the middle distance with little hooks which he flung out in front of him, and when they caught on, and he pulled out the result, he felt better. He was a sportsman, and not only in the field. He hit any one who disagreed with him, and was very angry if they hit him back. He hit the money-market with his judgment when he could, and when he couldn't, he hit it with his tongue. And all the time he hit the Government. It was a perpetual comfort to him in those shaky times to have that Government to hit. Whatever turned out wrong, whatever turned out right—there it was! To give it one—two—three, and watch it crawl away, was wonderfully soothing. Of a summer evening, sitting in the window of his club, having hit balls or bookies hard all day, how pleasant still to have that fellow Dash, and that fellow Blank, and all the ——y crew to hit still harder. He hit women, not, of course, with his fists, but with his philosophy. Women were made for the perfection of men; they had produced, nourished, and nursed him, and he now felt the necessity for them to comfort and satisfy him. When they had done that he felt no further responsibility in regard to them; to feel further responsibility was to be effeminate. The idea, for instance, that a spiritual feeling must underlie the physical was extravagant; and when a woman took another view, he took—if not actually, then metaphorically—a stick. He was almost Teutonic in that way. But the Government, the Government! Right and left, he hit it all the time. He had a rooted conviction that some day it would hit him back, and this naturally exasperated him. In the midst of danger to the game laws, of socialism, and the woman's movement, the only hope, almost the only comfort, lay in hitting the Government. For socialists were getting so near that he could only hit them now in clubs, music-halls, and other quite safe places; and the woman's movement might be trusted implicitly to hit itself. Thus, in the world arena there was nothing left but that godsend. Always a fair man, and of thoroughly good heart, he, of course, gave it credit for the same amount of generosity and good will that he felt present in his own composition. There was no extravagance in that; and any man who gave it more he deemed an ass.

He had heard of "the people," and, indeed, at times had seen and smelt them; it had sufficed. Some persons, he knew, were concerned about their condition and all that; but what good it would do him to share that concern he could not see. Fellows spoke of them as "poor devils," and so forth; to his mind they were "pretty good rotters," most of them—especially the working-man, who wanted something for nothing all the time, and grumbled when he got it. The more you gave him the more he wanted, and, if he were this ―― Government, instead of coddling the blighters up he would hit them one, and have done with it. Insurance, indeed; pensions; land reform; minimum wage—it was a bit too thick! They would soon be putting the beggars into glass cases, and labelling them "This side up."

Sometimes he dreamed of the time when he would have to ride for God and the king. But he strongly repelled, of course, any suggestion that he had been brought up to a belief in "caste." At his school he had once kicked a small scion of the royal family; this heroic action had dispersed in his mind once for all any notion that he was a snob. "Caste," indeed! There was no such thing in England nowadays. Had he not sung "The Leather Bottel" to an audience of dirty people in his school mission-hall, and—rather enjoyed it. It was not his fault that Labor was not satisfied. It was all those professional agitators, confound them! He himself was opposed to setting class against class. It was, however, ridiculous to imagine that he was going to hobnob with or take interest in people who weren't clean, who wore clothes with a disagreeable smell—people, moreover, who, in the most blatant way, showed him continually that they wanted what he had got. No, no! there were limits. Clean, at all events, any one could be—it was the *sine quâ non*. What with clothes, a man to look after them, baths, and so on, he himself spent at least two hundred a year on being clean, and even took risks with the thickness of his skin, from the way he rubbed and scrubbed it. A man could not be hard and healthy if he wasn't clean, and if the blighters were only hard and healthy they would not be bleating about their wants.

One could see him perhaps to the best advantage in lands like India, or Egypt, striding in the early morn over the purlieus of the desert, with his loping, strenuous step, scurried after by what looked like little dark and anxious women, carrying his golf-clubs; his eyes, with their look of out-facing Death, fixed on the ball that he had just hit so hard, intent on overtaking it and hitting it even harder next time. Did he at these times of worship ever pause to contemplate that vast and ancient plain where, in the distance, pyramids, those creatures of eternity, seemed to tremble in the sun haze? Did he ever feel an ecstatic wonder at the strange cry of immemorial peoples far-travelling the desert air; or look and marvel at those dark and anxious little children of old civilisations who pattered after him? Did he ever feel the majesty of those vast lonely sands and that vast lonely sky? Not he! He d——d well hit the ball, until his skin began to act; then, going in, took a bath, and rubbed himself. At such moments he felt perhaps more truly religious than at any other, for one naturally could not feel so fit and good on Sundays, with the necessity it imposed for extra eating, smoking, kneeling, and other sedentary occupations. Indeed, he had become perhaps a little distracted in religious matters. There seemed to be things in the Bible about turning the other cheek, and lilies of the field, about rich men and camels, and the poor in spirit, which did not go altogether with his religion. Still, of course, one remained in the English church, hit things, and hoped for the best.

Once his convictions nearly took a toss. It was on a ship, not as classy as it might have been, so that he was compelled to talk to people that he would not otherwise perhaps have noticed. Amongst such was a fellow with a short beard, coming from Morocco. This person was lean and brown, his eyes were extremely clear; he held himself very straight, and looked fit to jump over the moon. It seemed obvious that he hit a lot of things. One questioned him, therefore, with some interest as to what he had been hitting. The fellow had been hitting nothing, absolutely nothing. How on earth, then, did he keep himself so fit? Walking, riding, fasting, swimming, climbing mountains, writing books; hitting neither the Government nor golf balls! Never to hit anything; write books, tolerate the Government, and look like that! It was 'not done.' And the odd thing was, the fellow didn't seem to know or care whether he was fit or not. All the four days that the voyage lasted, with this infernal fellow under his very nose, he suffered. There was nothing to hit on board, and he himself did not feel very fit. However, on reaching Southampton and losing sight of his travelling acquaintance he soon regained his equanimity.

He often wondered what he would do when he passed the age of fifty; and felt more and more that he would either have to go into Parliament or take up the duties of a county magistrate. After that age there were certain kinds of balls and beasts that could no longer be hit with impunity, and if one was at all of an active turn of mind one must have substitutes. Marriage, no doubt, would do something for him, but not enough; his was a strenuous nature, and he intended to remain "hard" unto the end. To combine that with service to his country, especially if, incidentally, he could hit socialism and poachers, radicals, loafers, and the income tax—this seemed to him an ideal well worthy of his philosophy and life, so far. And with this in mind he lived on, his skin thickening, growing ever more and more perfect, more and more impervious to thought and feeling, to æstheticism, sympathy, and all the elements destructive of perfection. And thus—when his time has come there is every hope that he may die.

X.—The Competitor

He was given that way almost from his nursery days, for he could not even dress without racing his little brother in the doing up of little buttons, and being upset if he got one little button behind. At the age of eight he climbed all the trees of his father's garden and, arriving at their tops, felt a pang because the creatures left off so abruptly that he could not get any higher. He wrestled with anybody who did not mind rolling on the floor; and stayed awake once all night because he heard that one of his cousins was coming next day and was a year older than himself. It was not that he desired to see this cousin, to welcome, or give him a good time; he simply designed to race him in the kitchen-garden, and to wrestle with him afterward. It would be grand, he thought, to bump the head of some one a year older than himself. The cousin, however, was "scratched" at the last moment. It was a blow. At the age of ten he cut his head open against a swing, and so far forgot himself as to cry when he saw the blood flowing. To have missed such an opportunity of being superior to other small boys made an indelible mark on his soul, for, though he had not cried from pain, he had from fright, and felt he might have beaten both emotions, if only he had had proper warning.

His first term at school he came out top, after a terrific struggle; there was one other boy in the class. And term after term he went on coming out top, or very near it. He never knew what he was learning, but he knew that he beat other boys. He ran all the races he could, and played all the games; not because he enjoyed them, but because unless you did you could not win. He was considered almost a prize specimen.

He went to college in an exhausted condition, and for two years devoted himself to dandyism, designing to be the coolest, slackest, best-dressed man up. He almost was. But as that day approached when one must either beat or be beaten in learning by one's contemporaries, a fearful feeling beset him, and he rushed off to a crammer. For a whole year he poured the crammer's notes into his memory. What they were all about he had no notion, but his memory retained them just over that hot week when he sat writing for his life, twice a day. He would have received a First, had not an examiner who did not understand that examinations are simply held to determine who can beat whom, asked him in the living voice a question, to answer which required a knowledge of why there was an answer. He came down exhausted, and ate his dinners for the Bar. It was an occupation at which he could achieve no distinction save that of eating them faster than any other student; and for two whole years he merely devoted himself to trying to be the best amateur actor and the best shot in the land. His method of acting was based on nothing so flat as identification with the character he personified, but on the amount of laughter and applause that he could get in excess of that bestowed on any other member of the company. Nor did he shoot birds because he loved them, like a true sportsman, but because it was a pleasure to him to feel each day that he had shot or was going to shoot more than any one else who was shooting with him.

The time had now come for him to embrace his profession, and he did so like a true Briton, with his eye ever on the future. He perceived from the first that this particular race was longer than any race he had ever started for, and he began slowly, with a pebble in his mouth, husbanding his wind. The whole thing was extremely dry and extremely boring, but of course one had to get there before all those other fellows. And round and round he ran, increasing his speed almost imperceptibly, soon beginning to have his eye on the half-dozen who seemed dangerously likely to get there before him if he did not mind that eye. It cannot be said that he enjoyed his work, or cared for the money it brought him, for, what with getting through his day, and thinking of those other fellows who might be forging ahead of him, he had no time to spend money, or even to give it away. And so it began rolling up. One day, however, perceiving that he had quite a lot, the thought came to him that he ought to do something with it. And happening soon after to go into a picture-gallery, he bought a picture. He had not had it long before it seemed to him better than the picture of a friend who rather went in for them; and he thought, "I could easily beat him if I gave myself to it a little." And he did. It was fascinating to perceive, each time he bought, that his taste had improved, and was getting steadily ahead of his friend's taste; and, indeed, not only of his friend's, but of that of other people. He felt that soon he would have better taste than anybody, and he bought and bought. It was not that he cared for the pictures, for he really had not time or mind to give to them—set as he was on reaching eminence; but he dreamed of leaving them to the National Gallery as a monument to his taste, and final proof of superiority to his friend, after they were both gone.

About this time he took silk, sacrificing nearly half of his income. He would have preferred to wait longer, had he not perceived that if he did wait, his friends —— and —— and —— —— would be taking silk before him. And, since he meant to be a judge first, this must naturally be guarded against. The prospective loss of so much income made him for a moment restful and expansive, as if he felt that he had been pushed almost too far by his competitive genius; and so he found time to marry—it being the commencement of the long vacation. For six weeks he hardly thought of his friends —— and —— and —— ——, but near the end of September he was shocked back into a more normal frame of mind by the news that they also had been offered and had taken silk. It behoved him, he felt, to put his wife behind him and go back into harness. It would be just like those fellows to get ahead of him, if they could; and he curtailed his honeymoon by quite three weeks. Not two years, however, elapsed before it became clear to him that to keep his place he must enter Parliament. And against his own natural feelings, against even the inclinations of his country, he secured a seat at the general election and began sitting. What, then, was his chagrin to find that his friend ——, and his friend ——, and even his friend —— ——, had also secured seats, and were sitting when he got there! What with the courts, and what with 'the House,' he became lean and very yellow; and his wife complained. He determined to give her a child every year to keep her quiet; for he felt that he must have perfect peace in his home surroundings if he were to maintain his position in the great life race for which he had started, knowing that his friends —— and —— and —— —— would never hesitate to avail themselves of his ill health, to beat him. None of those wretched fellows were having so many children. He did not find his work in Parliament congenial; it seemed to him unreal. For he could not get his mind—firmly fixed on himself and the horizon—to believe that all those little measures which he was continually passing would benefit people with whose lives he really had not time or inclination to be familiar. When one had got up, prepared two cases, had breakfasted, walk down to the courts, sat there from half-past ten to four, walked to 'the House,' sat there a little longer than his friend —— —— (the worst of them), spoken if his friend —— had spoken, or if he thought his friend —— were going to speak, had dinner, prepared two cases, kissed his wife, mentally compared his last picture with that last one of his friend's, had a glass of barley-water, and gone to bed—when one had done all this, there really was not time for living his own life, much less any one else's. He sometimes thought he would have to give up doing so much; but that, of course, was out of the question, seeing that his friends would at once shoot ahead. He took "Vitogen" instead. They used his photograph, with the words, "It does wonders with me," coming out of his mouth, and on the opposite page they used a photograph of his friend —— ——, with the words, "I take a glass a day, and revel in it," coming out of his. On discovering this he increased the amount at some risk to two glasses, determined not to be outdone by that fellow.

He sometimes wondered whether, in the army, the church, the stock exchange, or in literature, he would not have had a more restful life; for he would by no means have admitted that he carried within himself the microbe of his own fate.

His natural love of beauty, for instance, inspired him when he saw a sunset, or a mountain, or even a sea, with the thought: How jolly it would be to look at it! But he had gradually become so reconciled to knowing he had not time for this that he never did. But if he had heard by any chance that his friend —— —— did find time to contemplate such natural beauties, he would certainly have contrived somehow to contemplate them too.

As the time approached for being made a judge he compared himself more and more carefully with his friends —— and —— ——. If they were appointed before him, it would be very serious for his prospects of ultimate pre-eminence. And it was with a certain relief, tempered with sorrow, that he heard one summer morning that his friend —— had fallen seriously ill, and was not expected to recover. He was assiduous in the expression of an anxiety that was quite genuine. His friend —— died as the courts rose. And all through that long vacation he thought continually of poor ——, and of his career cut so prematurely short. It was then that the idea came to him of capping his efforts by writing a book. He chose for subject, "The Evils of Competition in the Modern State," and devoted to it every minute he could spare during autumn months, fortunately bereft of Parliamentary duties. It would just, he felt make the difference between himself and his friends —— and —— ——, to a government essentially favourable to literary men. He finished it at Christmas, and arranged for a prompt publication. It was with a certain natural impatience that he read, two days later, of the approaching issue of a book by his friend —— ——, entitled, "Joy of Life, or the Cult of the Moment." What on earth the fellow was about to rush into print and on such a subject he was at a loss to understand! The book came out a week before his own. He read the reviews rather feverishly, for they were favourable. What to do now to recover his lead he hardly knew. If he had not been married it might have been possible to arrange something in that line with the daughter of an important personage; as it was, there was nothing for it but to part with his pictures to the National Gallery by way of a loan. And this he did, to the chagrin of his wife, about the middle of May. On the 1st of June he read in his Sunday paper that his friend —— —— had given his library outright to the British Museum. Some relief to the strain of his anxiety, however, was afforded in July by the unexpected accession of his friend —— to a peerage, through the death of a cousin. The estate attached was considerable. He felt that this friend at all events would not continue to struggle; he would surely recognise that he was removed from active life. His premonition was correct; and his friend —— —— and himself were left to fight it out alone.

That judge who had so long been expected to quit his judgeship did so for another world in the fourth week of the long vacation.

He hastened back to town at once. This was one of the most crucial moments of a crucial career. If appointed, he would be the youngest judge. But his friend —— —— was of the same age, the same politics, the same calibre in every way, and more robust. During those weeks of waiting, therefore, he grew perceptibly greyer. His joy knew only the bonds of a careful conceal-ment, when, at the beginning of October, he was appointed a judge of the High Court; for it was not till the following morning that he learned that his friend —— —— had also been appointed, the Government having decided to add one to the number of His Majesty's judges. Which of them had been made the extra judge he neither dared nor cared to inquire; but, setting his teeth, entered forthwith on his duties.

It cannot be pretended that he liked them; to like them one would have to take a profound, and, as it were, amateurish interest in equity and the lives of one's fellow-men. For this, of course, he had not time, having to devote all his energies to not having his judgments reversed, and watching the judg-ments of his friend —— ——. In the first year that fellow was upset in the Court of Appeal three times oftener than himself, and it came as a blow when the House of Lords so restored him that they came out equal. In other respects, of course, the life was something of a rest after that which he had led hitherto, and he watched himself carefully lest he might deteriorate, and be tempted to enjoy himself, steadily resisting every effort on the part of his friends and family to draw him into recreations other than those of din-ing out, playing golf, and improving his acquaintanceship with that Law of which he would require a perfect knowledge when he became Lord Chancel-lor. He never could quite make up his mind whether to be glad or sorry that his friend —— —— did not confine himself entirely to this curriculum.

At about this epoch he became so extremely moderate in his politics that neither party knew to which of them he belonged. It was a period of uncer-tainty when no man could say in whose hands power would be in, say, five or ten years' time, and instinctively he felt that he must look ahead. A moderate man stood perhaps the greater chance of steady and perpetual preferment, and he felt moderate, now that the spur of a necessary political activity was removed. It was a constant source of uneasiness to him that his friend —— —— had become so dark a horse that one could find out nothing about his political convictions; people, indeed, went so far as to say that the beggar had none.

He had not been a judge four years when an epidemic of influenza swept off three of His Majesty's judges, and sent one mad; and almost impercep-tibly he found himself sitting with his friend —— —— in the Court of Ap-peal. Having the fellow there under his eye day by day, he was able to study him, and noted with satisfaction that, though more robust, he was certainly of full and choleric temperament, and not too careful of himself. At once he began taking extra care of his own health, giving up wine, tobacco, and any other pleasure that he had left. For three years they sat there side by side, almost mechanically differing in their judgments; and then one morning the Prime Minister went and made his friend —— —— Lord Chief Justice, and himself only Master of the Rolls. The shock was very great. After a week's indisposition, he reset his teeth and decided to struggle on; his friend —— —— was not Lord Chancellor yet! Two more years passed, during which he unwillingly undermined his health by dining constantly in the highest social and political circles, and delivering longer and weightier judgments every day. His wife and children, who still had access to him at times, watched him with anxiety.

One morning they found him pacing up and down the dining-room with *The Times* newspaper in his hand, and every mark of cerebral excitement. His friend —— —— had made a speech at a certain banquet, in which he had hit the Government a nasty knock. It was now, of course, only a question of whether they would retain office till the Lord Chancellor, who was very shaky, dropped off. He dropped off in June, and they buried him in Westminster Abbey; his friend —— —— and himself being chief mourners. In the same week the Government was defeated. The state of his mind can now not well be imagined. In one week he lost five pounds that could not be spared. He stopped losing weight when the Government decided to hang on till the end of the session. On the 15th of July the Prime Minister sent for him, and offered him the Chancellorship. He accepted it, after first drawing attention to the superior claims of his friend —— ——. That evening, in the bosom of his family, he sat silent. A little smile played three times on his worn lips, and now and again his thin hand smoothed the parallel folds in his cheeks. His youngest daughter, moving to the bell behind his revered and beloved presence, heard him suddenly mutter, and bending hastily caught the precious words: "Pipped him on the post, by gum!"

He took up his final honours with the utmost ceremony. From that moment it was almost too noticeable how his powers declined. It was as if he had felt that, having won the race, he had nothing left to live for. Indeed, he only waited till his friend —— —— had received a slight stroke before, under doctor's orders, he laid down office. He dragged on for several years, writing his memoirs, but without interest in life; till one day, being drawn in his Bath-chair down the esplanade at Margate, he was brought to a standstill by another chair being drawn in the opposite direction. Letting his eye rest wearily on the occupant, he recognised his friend —— ——. How the fellow had changed; but not in nature, for he quavered out at once: "Hallo! It's you! By George! You look jolly bad!" Hearing those words, seeing that paralytic smile, a fire seemed suddenly relit within him. Compressing his lips, he answered nothing, and dug his Bath-chair man in the back. From that moment he regained his interest in life. If he could not outlive his friend —— —— it would be odd! And he set himself to do it, thinking of nothing else by day or night, and sending daily to inquire how his friend —— —— was. The fellow lived till New Year's Day, and died at two in the morning. They brought him the news at nine. A smile lighted up his parched and withered face; his old hands, clenched on the feeding-cup, relaxed; he fell back—dead. The shock of his old friend's death, they said, had been too much for him.

FOR LOVE OF BEASTS

§ 1.

We had left my rooms, and were walking briskly down the street towards the river, when my friend stopped before the window of a small shop and said:
"Gold-fish!"

I[1] looked at him very doubtfully; one had known him so long that one never looked at him in any other way.

"Can you imagine," he went on, "how any sane person can find pleasure in the sight of those swift things swimming for ever and ever in a bowl about twice the length of their own tails?"

"No," I said, "I cannot—though, of course, they're very pretty."

"That is, no doubt, the reason why they are kept in misery."

Again I looked at him; there is nothing in the world I distrust so much as irony.

"People don't think about these things," I said.

"You are right," he answered, "they do not. Let me give you some evidence of that…. I was travelling last spring in a far country, and made an expedition to a certain woodland spot. Outside the little forest inn I noticed a ring of people and dogs gathered round a grey animal rather larger than a cat. It had a sharp-nosed head too small for its body, and bright black eyes, and was moving restlessly round and round a pole to which it was tethered by a chain. If a dog came near, it hunched its bushy back and made a rush at him. Except for that it seemed a shy-souled, timid little thing. In fact, by its eyes, and the way it shrank into itself, you could tell it was scared of everything around. Now, there was a small, thin-faced man in a white jacket holding up a tub on end and explaining to the people that this was the little creature's habitat, and that it wanted to get back underneath; and, sure enough, when he held the tub within its reach, the little animal stood up at once on its hind legs and pawed, evidently trying to get the tub to fall down and cover it. The people all laughed at this; the man laughed too, and the little creature went on pawing. At last the man said: 'Mind your back-legs, Patsy!' and let the tub

---

1   For "I" read "almost any one."——J. G.

fall. The show was over. But presently another lot came up; the white-coated man lifted the tub, and it began all over again.

"'What is that animal?' I asked him.

"'A 'coon.'

"'How old?'

"'Three years—too old to tame.'

"'Where did you catch it?'

"'In the forest—lots of 'coons in the forest.'

"'Do they live in the open, or in holes?'

"'Up in the trees, sure; they only gits in the hollows when it rains.'

"'Oh! they live in the open? Then isn't it queer she should be so fond of her tub?'

"'Oh,' he said, 'she do that to git away from people!' and he laughed—a genial little man. 'She not like people and dogs. She too old to tame. She know *me*, though.'

"'I see,' I said. 'You take the tub off her, and show her to the people, and put it back again. Yes, she *would* know you!'

"'Yes,' he repeated, rather proudly, 'she know me—Patsy, Patsy! Presently, you bet, we catch lot more, and make a cage, and put them in.'

"He was gazing very kindly at the little creature, who on her grey hind legs was anxiously begging for the tub to come down and hide her, and I said: 'But isn't it rather a miserable life for this poor little devil?'

"He gave me a very queer look. 'There's lots of people,' he said—and his voice sounded as if I'd hurt him—'never gits a chance to see a 'coon'—and he dropped the tub over the racoon....

"Well! Can you conceive anything more pitiful than that poor little wild creature of the open, begging and begging for a tub to fall over it and shut out all the *light and air*? Doesn't it show what misery caged things have to go through?"

"But, surely," I said, "those other people would feel the same as you. The little white-coated man was only a servant."

He seemed to run them over in his memory. "Not one!" he answered slowly. "Not a single one! I am sure it never even occurred to them—why should it? They were there to enjoy themselves."

We walked in silence till I said:

"I can't help feeling that your little white-coated man was acting good-heartedly according to his lights."

"Quite! And after all what are the sufferings of a racoon compared with the enlargement of the human mind?"

"Don't be extravagant! You know he didn't mean to be cruel."

"Does a man ever mean to be cruel? He merely makes or keeps his living; but to make or keep his living he will do anything that does not absolutely prick to his heart through the skin of his indolence or his obtuseness."

"I think," I said, "that you might have expressed that less cynically, even if it's true."

"Nothing that's true is cynical, and nothing that is cynical is true. Indifference to the suffering of beasts always comes from over-absorption in our own comfort."

"Absorption, not over-absorption, perhaps."

"Ha! Let us see that! Very soon after seeing the racoon I was staying at the most celebrated health resort of that country, and, walking in its grounds, I came on an aviary. In the upper cages were canaries, and in the lower cage a splendid hawk. It was as large as our buzzard hawk, brown-backed and winged, light underneath, and with the finest dark-brown eyes of any bird I ever saw. The cage was quite ten feet each way—a noble allowance for the very soul of freedom! The bird had every luxury. There was water, and a large piece of raw meat that hadn't been touched. Yet it was never still for a moment, flying from perch to perch, and dropping to the ground again and again so lightly, to run, literally run, up to the bars to see if perhaps—they were not there. Its face was as intelligent as any dog's——"

My friend muttered something I couldn't catch, and then went on:

"That afternoon I took the drive for which one visits that hotel, and it occurred to me to ask my chauffeur what kind of hawk it was. 'Well,' he said, 'I ain't just too sure what it is they've got caged up now; they changes 'em so often.'

"'Do you mean,' I said, 'that they die in captivity?'

"'Yes,' he answered, 'them big birds soon gits moulty and go off.' Well, when I paid my bill I went up to the semblance of proprietor—it was one of these establishments where the only creature responsible is 'Co.'—and I said:

"'I see you keep a hawk out there?'

"'Yes. Fine bird. Quite an attraction!'

"'People like to look at it?'

"'Just so. They're uncommon—that sort.'

"'Well,' I said 'I call it cruel to keep a hawk shut up like that.'

"'Cruel? Why? What's a hawk, anyway—cruel devils enough!'

"'My dear sir,' I said, 'they earn their living just like men, without caring for other creatures' sufferings. You are not shut up, apparently, for doing that. Good-bye.'"

As he said this, my friend looked at me, and added:

"You think that was a lapse of taste. What would *you* have said to a man who cloaked the cruelty of his commercial instincts by blaming a hawk for being what Nature had made him?"

There was such feeling in his voice that I hesitated long before answering.

"Well," I said, at last, "in England, anyway, we only keep such creatures in captivity for scientific purposes. I doubt if you could find a single instance nowadays of its being done just as a commercial attraction."

He stared at me.

"Yes," he said, "we do it publicly and scientifically, to enlarge the mind. But let me put to you this question. Which do you consider has the larger mind—the man who has satisfied his idle curiosity by staring at all the caged animals of the earth, or the man who has been brought up to feel that to keep such indomitable creatures as hawks and eagles, wolves and panthers, shut up, to gratify mere curiosity, is a dreadful thing?"

To that singular question I knew not what to answer. At last I said:

"I think you underrate the pleasure they give. We English are so awfully fond of animals!"

§ 2.

We had entered Battersea Park by now, and since my remark about our love of beasts we had not spoken. A wood-pigeon which had been strutting before us just then flew up into a tree and began puffing out its breast. Seeking to break the silence, I said:

"Pigeons are so complacent."

My friend smiled in his dubious way, and answered:

"Do you know the 'blue rock?'"

"No."

"Ah! there you have a pigeon who has less complacency than any living thing. You see, it depends on circumstances. Suppose, for instance, that we happened to keep Our Selves—perhaps the most complacent class of human beings—in a large space enclosed by iron railings, feeding them up carefully, until their natural instincts caused them to run up and down at a considerable speed from side to side of the enclosure. And suppose when we noticed that they had attained the full speed and strength of their legs we took them out, holding them gingerly in order that they might not become exhausted by struggling, and placed them in little tin compartments so dark and stuffy that they would not care of their own accord to stay there, and then stood back about thirty paces with a shot gun and pressed a spring which let the tin compartment collapse. And then, as each one of Our Selves ran out, we let fly with the right barrel and peppered him in the tail, whereon, if he fell, we sent a dog out to fetch him in by the slack of his breeches, and after holding him idly for a minute by the neck we gave it a wring round; or, if he did not fall, we prayed Heaven at once and let fly with the left barrel. Do you think in these circumstances Our Selves would be complacent?"

"Don't be absurd!" I said.

"Very well," he replied, "I will come to 'blue rocks'—do you still maintain that they are so complacent as to deserve their fate?"

"I don't know—I know nothing about their fate."

"What the eyes do not swallow, the heart does not throw up! There are other places, but—have you been to Monte Carlo?"

"No, and I should never think of going there."

"Oh, well," he answered, "it's a great place; but there's just one little thing about it, and that's in the matter of those 'blue rocks.' You'll agree, I suppose, that one can't complain of people amusing themselves in any way they like so long as they hurt no one but themselves——"

I caught him up: "I don't agree at all."

He smiled: "Yours is perhaps the English point of view. Still——"

"It's more important that they shouldn't hurt themselves than that they shouldn't hurt pigeons, if that's what you're driving at," I said.

"There wouldn't appear to you, I suppose, to be any connection in the matter?"

"I tell you," I repeated, "I know nothing about pigeon-shooting!"

He stared very straight before him.

"Imagine," he said, "a blue sea, and a half-circle of grass, with a low wall. Imagine on that grass five traps, from which lead paths—like the rays of a star—to the central point on the base of that half-circle. And imagine on that central point a gentleman with a double-barrelled gun, another man, and a retriever dog. And imagine one of those traps opening, and a little dazed grey bird (not a bit like that fellow you saw just now) emerge and fly perhaps six yards. And imagine the sound of the gun and the little bird dipping in its flight, but struggling on. And imagine the sound of the gun again and the little bird falling to the ground and wriggling on along it. And imagine the retriever dog run forward and pick it up and walk slowly back with it, still quivering, in his mouth. Or imagine, once in a way, the little bird drop dead as a stone at the first sound. Or imagine again that it winces at the shots, yet carries on over the boundary, to fall into the sea. Or—but this very seldom— imagine it wing up and out, unhurt, to the first freedom it has ever known. My friend, the joke is this: To the man who lets no little bird away to freedom comes much honour, and a nice round sum of money! Do you still think there is no connection?"

"Well," I said, "it doesn't sound too sportsmanlike. And yet, I suppose, looking at it quite broadly, it does minister in a sort of way to the law of the survival of the fittest."

"In which species—man or pigeon?"

"The sportsman is necessary to the expansion of Empire. Besides, you must remember that one does not expect high standards at Monte Carlo."

He looked at me. "Do you never read any sporting paper?" he asked.

"No."

"Did you ever hunt the carted stag?"

"No, I never did."

"Well, you've been coursing, anyway."

"Certainly; but there's no comparing that with pigeon-shooting."

"In coursing I admit," he said, "there's pleasure to the dogs, and some chance for the hare, who, besides, is not in captivity. Also that where there is no coursing there are few hares, in these days. And yet——"; he seemed to fall into a reverie.

Then, looking at me in a queer, mournful sort of way, he said suddenly:

"I don't wish to attack that sport, when there are so many much worse, but by way of showing you how liable all these things are to contribute to the improvement of our species I will tell you a little experience of my own. When I was at college I was in a rather sporting set; we hunted, and played at racing, and loved to be '*au courant*' with all that sort of thing. One year it so happened that the uncle of one of us won the Waterloo Cup with a greyhound whose name was—never mind. We became at once ardent lovers of the sport of coursing, consumed by the desire to hold a Waterloo Cup Meeting in miniature, with rabbits for hares and our own terriers for greyhounds. Well, we held it; sixteen of us nominating our dogs. Now kindly note that of those sixteen eight at least were members of the aristocracy, and all had been at public schools of standing and repute. For the purposes of our meeting, of course, we required fifteen rabbits caught and kept in bags. These we ordered of a local blackguard, with a due margin over to provide against such of the rabbits as might die of fright before they were let out, or be too terrified to run after being loosed. We made the fellow whose uncle had won the Waterloo Cup judge, apportioned among ourselves the other officers, and assembled—the judge on horseback, in case a rabbit might happen to run, say, fifty yards. Assembled with us were many local cads, two fourth-rate bookies, our excited, yapping terriers, and twenty-four bagged rabbits. The course was cleared. Two of us advanced, holding our terriers by the loins; the judge signed that he was ready; the first rabbit was turned down. It crept out of the bag, and squatted, close to the ground, with its ears laid back. The local blackguard stirred it with his foot. It crept two yards, and squatted closer. All the terriers began shrieking their little souls out, all the cads began to yell, but the rabbit did not move—its heart, you see, was broken. At last the local blackguard took it up and wrung its neck. After that some rabbits ran, and some did not, till all were killed! The terrier of one of us was judged victor by him whose uncle had won the Waterloo Cup; and we went back to our colleges to drink everybody's health. Now, my friend, mark! We were sixteen decent youths, converted by infection into sixteen rabbit-catching cads. Two of us are dead; but the rest of us—what do we think of it now? I tell you this little incident, to confirm you in your feeling that pigeon-shooting, coursing, and the like, tend to improve our species, even here in England."

§ 3.

Before I could comment on my friend's narrative we were spattered with mud by passing riders, and stopped to repair the damage to our coats.

"Jolly for my new coat!" I said. "Do you notice, by the way, that they are cutting men's tails longer this spring? More becoming to a fellow, I think."

He raised those quizzical eyebrows of his and murmured:

"And horses' tails shorter. Did you see those that passed just now?"

"No."

"There were none!"

"Nonsense!" I said. "My dear fellow, you really are obsessed about beasts! They were just ordinary."

"Quite—a few scrubby hairs, and a wriggle."

"Now, please," I said, "don't begin to talk of the cruelty of docking horses' tails, and tell me a story of an old horse in a pond."

"No," he answered, "for I should have to invent that. What I was going to say was this: Which do you think the greater fools in the matter of fashion—men or women?"

"Oh! Women."

"Why?"

"There's always some sense at the bottom of men's fashions."

"Even of docking tails?"

"You can't compare it, anyway," I said, "with such a fashion as the wearing of 'aigrettes.' That's a cruel fashion if you like."

"Ah! But you see," he said, "the women who wear them are ignorant of its cruelty. If they were not, they would never wear them. No gentlewoman wears them, now that the facts have come out."

"What is that you say?" I remarked.

He looked at me gravely.

"Do you mean to tell me," he asked, "that any woman of gentle instincts, who *knows* that the 'aigrette,' as they call it, is a nuptial plume sported by the white egret only during the nesting season—and that, in order to obtain it, the mother-birds are shot, and that, after their death, practically all their young die from hunger and exposure—do you mean to tell me that any gentlewoman, knowing that, wears them? Why! most women are mothers themselves! What would they think of gods who shot women with babies in arms for the sake of obtaining their white skins or their crop of hair to wear on their heads, eh?"

"But, my dear fellow," I said, "you see these plumes about all over the place!"

"Only on people who don't mind wearing imitation stuff."

I gaped at him.

"You need not look at me like that," he said. "A woman goes into a shop. She knows that real 'aigrettes' mean, killing mother-birds and starving all their nestlings. Therefore, if she's a real gentlewoman she doesn't ask for a real 'aigrette.' But still less does she ask to be supplied with an imitation article so good that people will take her for the wearer of the real thing. I put it to you, would she want to be known as an encourager of such a practice? You can never have seen a *lady* wearing an 'aigrette.'"

"What!" I said. "What?"

"So much for the woman who knows about 'aigrettes,'" he went on. "Now for the woman who doesn't. Either, when she is told these facts about 'aigrettes' she sets them down as 'hysterical stuff,' or she is simply too 'out of it' to know anything. Well, she goes in and asks for an 'aigrette.' Do you think they sell her the real thing—I mean, of course, in England—knowing that it involves the shooting of mother-birds at breeding time? I put it to you: Would they?"

His inability to grasp the real issues astonished me, and I said:

"You and I happen to have read the evidence about 'aigrettes' and the opinion of the House of Lords Committee that the feathers of egrets imported into Great Britain are obtained by killing the birds during the breeding season; but you don't suppose, do you, that people whose commercial interests are bound up with the selling of 'aigrettes' are going to read it, or believe it if they do read it?"

"That," he answered, "is cynical, if you like. I feel sure that, in England, people do not sell suspected articles about which there has been so much talk and inquiry as there has been about 'aigrettes' without examining in good faith into the facts of their origin. No, believe me, none of the 'aigrettes' sold in England can have grown on birds."

"This is fantastic," I said. "Why! if what you're saying is true, then—then real 'aigrettes' are all artificial; but that—that would be cheating!"

"Oh, no!" he said. "You see, 'aigrettes' are in fashion. The word 'real' has therefore become parliamentary. People don't want to be cruel, but they must have 'real' aigrettes. So, all these 'aigrettes' are 'real,' unless the customer has a qualm, and then they are 'real imitation aigrettes.' We are a highly civilised people!"

"That is very clever," I said, "but how about the statistics of real egret plumes imported into this country?"

He answered like a flash: "Oh, those, of course, are only brought here to be exported again at once to countries where they do not mind confessing to cruelty; yes, all exported, except—well, *those that aren't!*"

"Oh!" I said: "I see! You have been speaking ironically all this time."

"Have you grasped that?" he answered. "Capital!" After that we walked in silence.

"The fact is," I said, presently, "ordinary people, shopmen and customers alike, never bother their heads about such things at all."

"Yes," he replied sadly, "they take the line of least resistance. It is just that which gives Fashion its chance to make such fools of them."

"You have yet to prove that it does make fools of them."

"I thought I had; but no matter. Take horses' tails—what's left of them—do you defend that fashion?"

"Well," I said, "I——"

"Would you if you were a horse?"

"If you mean that I am a donkey——?"

"Oh, no! Not at all!"

"It's going too far," I said, "to call docking cruel."

"Personally," he answered, "I don't think it is going too far. It's painful in itself, and Heaven alone knows what irritation horses have to suffer from flies through being tailless. I admit that it saves a little brushing, and that some people are under the delusion that it averts carriage accidents. But put cruelty and utility aside, and look at it from the point of view of fashion. Can anybody say it doesn't spoil a horse's looks?"

"You know perfectly well," I said, "that many people think it smartens him up tremendously. They regard a certain kind of horse as nothing with a tail; just as some men are nothing with beards."

"The parallel with man does not hold, my friend. We are not shaved—with or against our wills—by demi-gods!"

"Exactly! And isn't that in itself an admission that we are superior to beasts, and have a right to some say in their appearance?"

"I will not," he answered, "for one moment allow that men are superior to horses in point of looks. Take yourself, or any other personable man, and stand him up against a thoroughbred and ask your friends to come and look. How much of their admiration do you think you will get?"

It was not the sort of question I could answer.

"I am not speaking at random," he went on; "I have seen the average lord walking beside the average winner of the Derby." He cackled disagreeably.

"But it's just on this point of looks that people defend docking," I said. "They breed the horses, and have a right to their own taste. Many people dislike long swishy appendages."

"And bull-terriers, or Yorkshires, or Great Danes, with natural ears; and fox-terriers and spaniels with uncut tails; and women with merely the middles so small as Nature gave them?"

"If you're simply going to joke——"

"I never was more serious. The whole thing is of a piece, and summed up in the word 'smart,' which you used just now. That word, sir, is the guardian angel of all fashions, and if you don't mind my saying so, fashions are the guardian angels of vulgarity. Now, a horse is not a vulgar animal, and I can never get away from the thought that to dock his tail must hurt his feelings of refinement."

"Well, if that's all, I dare say he'll get over it."

"But will the man who does it?"

"You must come with me to the Horse Show," I said, "and look at the men who have to do with horses; then you'll know if such a thing as docking the tails of these creatures can do them harm or not. And, by the way, you talk of refinement and vulgarity. What is your test? Where is the standard? It's all a matter of taste."

"You want me to define these things?" he asked.

"Yes."

"Very well! Do you believe in what we call the instincts of a gentleman?"

"Of course."

"Such as—the instinct to be self-controlled; not to be rude or intolerant; not to 'slop-over'; not to fuss, nor to cry out; to hold your head up, so that people refrain from taking liberties; to be ready to do things for others, to be chary of asking others to do things for you, and grateful when they do them?"

"Yes," I said, "all these I believe in."

"What central truth do you imagine that these instincts come from?"

"Well, they're all such a matter of course—I don't think I ever considered."

"If by any chance," he replied, "you ever do, you will find they come from an innate worship of balance, of the just mean; an inborn reverence for due proportion, a natural sense of harmony and rhythm, and a consequent mistrust of extravagance. What is a bounder? Just a man without sufficient sense of proportion to know that he is not so important in the scheme of things as he thinks he is!"

"You are right there!"

"Very well. Refinement is a quality of the individual who has—and conforms to—a true (not a conventional) sense of proportion; and vulgarity is either the natural conduct of people without that sense of proportion, or of people who imitate and reproduce the tricks of refinement wholesale, without any real feeling for proportion; or again, it is mere conscious departure from the sense of proportion for the sake of cutting a dash."

"Ah!" I said; "and to which of these kinds of vulgarity is the fashion of docking horses' tails a guardian angel?"

"Imagine," he answered gravely, "that you dock your horse's tail. You are either horribly deficient in feeling for a perfectly proportioned horse, or you imitate what you believe—goodness knows why—to be the refined custom of docking horses' tails, without considering the question of proportion at all."

"Yes," I said; "but what makes so many people do it, if there isn't something in it, either useful or ornamental?"

"Because people as a rule do not love proportion; they love the grotesque. You have only to look at their faces, which are very good indications of their souls."

"You have begged the question," I said. "Who are you to say that the perfect horse is not the horse——?"

"With the imperfect tail?"

"Imperfect? Again, you're begging."

"As Nature made it, then. Oh!" he went on with vehemence, "think of the luxury of having your own tail. Think of the cool swish of it. Think of the real beauty of it! Think of the sheer hideousness of all that great front balanced behind by a few scrub hairs and a wriggle! It became 'smart' to dock horses' tails; and smart to wear 'aigrettes.' 'Smart'—'neat'—'efficient'—for all except the horse and the poor egrets."

"Your argument," I said, "is practically nothing but æsthetics."

He fixed his eyes upon my hat.

"Well," he said slowly. "I admit that neither on horse nor on man would long tails go at all well with that bowler hat of yours. Odd how all of a piece taste is! From a man's hat, or a horse's tail, we can reconstruct the age we live in, like that scientist, you remember, who reconstructed a mastodon from its funny-bone."

The thought went sharply through my head: Is his next tirade to be on mastodons? Till I remembered with relief that the animal was extinct, at all events in England.

§ 4.

With but little further talk we had nearly reached my rooms, when he said abruptly:

"A lark! Can't you hear it? Over there, in that wretched little goldfish shop again."

But I could only hear the sounds of traffic.

"It's your imagination," I said. "It really is too lively on the subject of birds and beasts."

"I tell you," he persisted, "there's a caged lark there. Very likely half-a-dozen."

"My dear fellow," I said, "suppose there are! We could go and buy them and set them free, but it would only encourage the demand. Or we could assault the shopmen. Do you recommend that?"

"I don't joke on this subject," he answered shortly.

"But surely," I said, "if we can't do anything to help the poor things we had better keep our ears from hearing."

"And our eyes shut? Suppose we all did that, what sort of world should we be living in?"

"Very much the same as now, I expect."

"Blasphemy! Rank, hopeless blasphemy!"

"Please don't exaggerate!"

"I am not. There is only one possible defence of that attitude, and it's this: The world is—and was deliberately meant to be—divided into two halves: the half that suffers and the half that benefits by that suffering."

"Well?"

"Is it so?"

"Perhaps."

"You acquiesce in that definition of the world's nature? Very well, if you belong to the first half you are a poor-spirited creature, consciously acquiescing in your own misery. If to the second, you are a brute, consciously acquiescing in your own happiness, at the expense of others. Well, which are you?"

"I have not said that I belong to either."

"There are only two halves to a whole. No, my friend, disabuse yourself once for all of that cheap and comfortable philosophy of shutting your eyes to what you think you can't remedy, unless you are willing to be labelled 'brute.' 'He who is not with me is against me,' you know."

"Well," I said, "after that, perhaps you'll be good enough to tell me what I can do by making myself miserable over things I can't help?"

"I will," he answered. "In the first place, kindly consider that you are not living in a private world of your own. Everything you say and do and think has its effect on everybody around you. For example, if you feel, and say loudly enough, that it is an infernal shame to keep larks and other wild songbirds in cages, you will infallibly infect a number of other people with that sentiment, and in course of time those people who feel as you do will become so numerous that larks, thrushes, blackbirds, and linnets will no longer be caught and kept in cages. Whereas, if you merely think: 'Oh! this is dreadful, quite too dreadful, but, you see, I can do nothing; therefore consideration for myself and others demands that I shall stop my ears and hold my tongue,' then, indeed, nothing will ever be done, and larks, blackbirds, etc., will continue to be caught and prisoned. How do you imagine it ever came about that bears and bulls and badgers are no longer baited; cocks no longer openly encouraged to tear each other in pieces; donkeys no longer beaten to a pulp? Only by people going about and shouting out that these things made them uncomfortable. How did it come about that more than half the population of this country are not still classed as 'serfs' under the law? Simply because a few of our ancestors were made unhappy by seeing their fellow-creatures owned and treated like dogs, and roundly said so—in fact, were not ashamed to be sentimental humanitarians like me."

"That is all obvious. But my point is that there is moderation in all things, and a time for everything."

"By your leave," he said, "there is little moderation desirable when we are face to face with real suffering, and, as a general rule, no time like the present."

"But there is, as you were saying just now, such a thing as a sense of proportion. I cannot see that it's my business to excite myself about the caging of larks when there are so many much greater evils."

"Forgive my saying so," he answered, "but if, when a caged lark comes under your nose, excitement does not take hold of you, with or against your will, there is mighty little chance of your getting excited about anything. For, consider what it means to be a caged lark—what pining and misery for that little creature, which only lives for its life up in the blue. Consider what blasphemy against Nature, and what an insult to all that is high and poetic in man, it is to cage such an exquisite thing of freedom!"

"You forget that it is done out of love for the song—to bring it into towns where people can't otherwise hear it."

"It is done for a living—and that people without imagination may squeeze out of unhappy creatures a little gratification!"

"It is not a crime to have no imagination."

"No, sir; but neither is the lack of it a thing to pride oneself on, or pass by in silence, when it inflicts suffering."

"I am not defending the custom of caging larks."

"No; but you are responsible for its continuance."

"I?"

"You and all those other people who believe in minding their own business."

"Really," I said; "you must not attack people on that ground. We cannot all be busybodies!"

"The saints forbid!" he answered. "But when a thing exists which you really abhor—as you do this—I do wish you would consider a little whether, in letting it strictly alone, you are minding your own business on principle, or because it is so jolly comfortable to do so."

"Speaking for myself——"

"Yes," he broke in; "quite! But let me ask you one thing: Have you, as a member of the human race, any feeling that you share in the advancement of its gentleness, of its sense of beauty and justice—that, in proportion as the human race becomes more lovable and lovely, you too become more lovable and lovely?"

"Naturally."

"Then is it not your business to support all that you feel makes for that advancing perfection?"

"I don't say that it isn't."

"In that case it is *not* your business to stop your ears, and shut your eyes, and hold your tongue, when you come across wild song-birds caged."

But we had reached my rooms.

"Before I go in," I said, "there is just one little thing I've got to say to you: Don't you think that, for a man with your 'sense of proportion,' you exaggerate the importance of beasts and their happiness?"

He looked at me for a long time without speaking, and when he did speak it was in a queer, abstracted voice:

"I have often thought over that," he said, "and honestly I don't believe I do. For I have observed that before men can be gentle and broad-minded with each other, they are always gentle and broad-minded about beasts. These dumb things, so beautiful—even the plain ones—in their different ways, and so touching in their dumbness, do draw us to magnanimity, and help the wings of our hearts to grow. No; I don't think I exaggerate, my friend. Most surely I don't want to; for there is no disservice one can do to all these help-less things so great as to ride past the hounds, to fly so far in front of public feeling as to cause nausea and reaction. But I feel that most of us, deep down, really love these furred and feathered creatures that cannot save themselves from us—that are like our own children, because they are helpless; that are in a way sacred, because in them we watch, and through them we understand, those greatest blessings of the earth—Beauty and Freedom. They give us so much, they ask nothing from us. What can we do in return but spare them all the suffering we can? No, my friend; I do not think—whether for their sakes or our own—that I exaggerate."

When we had said those words he turned away and left me standing there.

REVERIE OF A SPORTSMAN

I set out one morning in late August, with some potted grouse sandwiches in one pocket and a magazine in the other, for a tramp toward Causdon. I had not been in that particular part of the moor since I used to go snipe-shooting there as a boy—my first introduction, by the way, to sport. It was a very lovely day, almost too hot; and I never saw the carpet of the moor more exquisite—heather, fern, the silvery white cotton grass, dark peat turves, and green bog-moss, all more than customarily clear in hue under a very blue sky. I walked till two o'clock, then sat down in a little scoop of valley by a thread of stream, which took its rise from an awkward looking bog at the top. It was wonderfully quiet. A heron rose below me and flapped away; and while I was eating my potted grouse I heard the harsh cheep of a snipe, and caught sight of the twisting bird vanishing against the line of sky above the bog. "That must have been one of the bogs we used to shoot," I thought; and having finished my snack of lunch, I rolled myself a cigarette, opened the magazine, and idly turned its pages. I had no serious intention of reading—the calm and silence were too seductive, but my attention became riveted by an exciting story of some man-eating lions, and I read on till I had followed the adventure to the death of the two ferocious brutes, and found my cigarette actually burning my fingers. Crushing it out against the dampish roots of the heather, I lay back with my eyes fixed on the sky, thinking of nothing.

Suddenly I became conscious that between me and that sky a leash of snipe high up were flighting and twisting and gradually coming lower; I appeared, indeed, to have a sort of attraction for them. They would dash toward each other, seem to exchange ideas, and rush away again, like flies that waltz together for hours in the centre of a room. As they came lower and lower over me I could almost swear I heard them whisper to each other with their long bills, and presently I absolutely caught what they were saying: "Look at him! The ferocious brute! Oh, look at him!"

Amazed at such an extraordinary violation of all the laws of Nature, I began to rub my ears, when I distinctly heard the "Go-back, go-back" of an old cock grouse, and, turning my head cautiously, saw him perched on a heathery knob within twenty yards of where I lay. Now, I knew very well that all efforts to introduce grouse on Dartmoor have been quite unsuccessful, since for some reason connected with the quality of the heather, the nature of the soil, or the over-mild dampness of the air, this king of game birds most unfortunately refuses to become domiciled there; so that I could hardly credit my senses. But suddenly I heard him also: "Look at him! Go back! The ferocious brute! Go back!" He seemed to be speaking to something just below; and there, sure enough, was the first hare I had ever seen out on the full of the moor. I have always thought a hare a jolly beast, and not infrequently felt sorry when I rolled one over; it has a way of crying like a child if not killed outright. I confess, then, that in hearing it, too, whisper: "Look at him! The ferocious brute! Oh, look at him!" I experienced the sensation that comes over one when one has not been quite fairly treated. Just at that moment, with a warm stirring of the air, there pitched within six yards of me a magnificent old black-cock—the very spit of that splendid fellow I shot last season at Balnagie, whose tail my wife now wears in her hat. He was accompanied by four grey hens, who, settling in a semi-circle, began at once: "Look at him! Look at him! The ferocious brute! Oh, look at him!" At that moment I say with candour that I regretted the many times I have spared grey hens with the sportsmanlike desire to encourage their breed.

For several bewildered minutes after that I could not turn my eyes without seeing some bird or other alight close by me: more and more grouse, and black game, pheasants, partridges—not only the excellent English bird, but the very sporting Hungarian variety—and that unsatisfactory red-legged Frenchman which runs any distance rather than get up and give you a decent shot at him. There were woodcock too, those twisting delights of the sportsman's heart, whose tiny wing-feather trophies have always given me a distinct sensation of achievement when pinned in the side of my shooting-cap; wood-pigeons too, very shy and difficult, owing to the thickness of their breast-feathers—and, after all, only coming under the heading "sundry"; wild duck, with their snaky dark heads, that I have shot chiefly in Canada, lurking among rushes in twilight at flighting time—a delightful sport, exciting, as the darkness grows; excellent eating too, with red pepper and sliced oranges in oil! Certain other sundries kept coming also; landrails, a plump, delicious little bird; green and golden plover; even one of those queer little creatures, moorhens, that always amuse one by their quick, quiet movements, plaintive note, and quaint curiosity, though not really, of course, fit to shoot, with their niggling flight and fishy flavour! Ptarmigan, too, a bird I admire very much, but have only once or twice succeeded in bringing down, shy and scarce as it is in Scotland. And, side by side, the alpha and omega of the birds to be shot in these islands, a capercailzie and a quail. I well remember shooting the latter in a turnip-field in Lincolnshire—a scrap of a bird, the only one I ever saw in England. Apart from the pleasurable sensation at its rarity, I recollect feeling that it was almost a mercy to put the little thing out of its loneliness. It ate very well. There, too, was that loon or northern diver that I shot with a rifle off Denman Island as it swam about fifty yards from the shore. Handsome plumage; I still have the mat it made. One bird only seemed to refuse to alight, remaining up there in the sky, and uttering continually that trilling cry which makes it perhaps the most spiritual of all birds that can be eaten—I mean, of course, the curlew. I certainly never shot one. They fly, as a rule, very high and seem to have a more than natural distrust of the human being. This curlew—ah! and a blue rock (I have always despised pigeon-shooting)—were the only two winged creatures that one can shoot for sport in this country that did not come and sit round me.

There must have been, I should say, as many hundred altogether as I have killed in my time—a tremendous number. They sat in a sort of ring, moving their beaks from side to side, just as I have seen penguins doing on the films that explorers bring back from the Antarctic; and all the time repeating to each other those amazing words: "Look at him! The ferocious brute! Oh, look at him!"

Then, to my increased astonishment, I saw behind the circles of the birds a number of other animals besides the hare. At least five kinds of deer—the red, the fallow, the roe, the common deer, whose name I've forgotten, which one finds in Vancouver Island, and the South African springbok, that swarm in from the Karoo at certain seasons, among which I had that happy week once in Namaqualand, shooting them from horseback after a gallop to cut them off—very good eating as camp fare goes, and making nice rugs if you sew their skins together. There, too, was the hyena I missed, probably not altogether; but he got off, to my chagrin—queer-looking brute! Rabbits of course had come—hundreds and hundreds of them. If—like everybody else—I've done such a lot of it, I can't honestly say I've ever cared much for shooting rabbits, though the effect is neat enough when you get them just right and they turn head over heels—and anyway, the prolific little brutes have to be kept down. There, too, actually was my wild ostrich—the one I galloped so hard after, letting off my Winchester at half a mile, only to see him vanish over the horizon. Next him was the bear whose lair I came across at the Nanaimo Lakes. How I did lurk about to get that fellow! And, by Jove! close to him, two cougars. I never got a shot at them, never even saw one of the brutes all the time I was camping in Vancouver Island, where they lie flat along the branches over your head, waiting to get a chance at deer, sheep, dog, pig, or anything handy. But they had come now sure enough, glaring at me with their greenish cats'-eyes—powerful-looking creatures! And next them sat a little meerkat—not much larger than a weasel—without its head! Ah yes!—that trial shot, as we trekked out from Rous's farm, and I wanted to try the little new rifle I had borrowed. It was sitting over its hole fully seventy yards from the wagon, quite unconscious of danger. I just took aim and pulled; and there it was, without its head, fallen across its hole. I remember well how pleased our "boys" were. And I too! Not a bad little rifle, that!

Outside the ring of beasts I could see foxes moving, not mixing with the stationary creatures, as if afraid of suggesting that I had shot them, instead of being present at their deaths in the proper fashion. One, quite a cub, kept limping round on three legs—the one, no doubt, whose pad was given me, out cubbing, as a boy. I put that wretched pad in my hat-box, and forgot it, so that I was compelled to throw the whole stinking show away. There were quite a lot of grown foxes; it certainly showed delicacy on their part, not sitting down with the others. There was really a tremendous crowd of creatures altogether by this time! I should think every beast and bird I ever shot, or even had a chance of killing, must have been there, and all whispering: "Look at him! The ferocious brute! Oh, look at him!"

Animal lover, as every true sportsman is, those words hurt me. If there is one thing on which we sportsmen pride ourselves, and legitimately, it is a humane feeling toward all furred and feathered creatures—and, as every one knows, we are foremost in all efforts to diminish their unnecessary sufferings.

The corroboree about me which they were obviously holding became, as I grew used to their manner of talking, increasingly audible. But it was the quail's words that I first distinguished.

"He certainly ate me," he said; "said I was good, too!"

"I do not believe"—this was the first hare speaking—"that he shot me for that reason; he did shoot me, and I was jugged, but he wouldn't touch me. And the same day he shot eleven brace of partridges, didn't he?" Twenty-two partridges assented. "And he only ate two of you all told—that proves he didn't want us for food."

The hare's words had given me relief, for I somehow disliked intensely the gluttonous notion conveyed by the quail that I shot merely in order to devour the result. Any one with the faintest instincts of a sportsman will bear me out in this.

When the hare had spoken there was a murmur all round. I could not at first make out its significance, till I heard one of the cougars say: "We kill only when we want to eat"; and the bear, who, I noticed, was a lady, added: "No bear kills anything she cannot devour"; and, quite clear, I caught the quacking words of a wild duck. "We eat every worm we catch, and we'd eat more if we could get them."

Then again from the whole throng came that shivering whisper: "Look at him! The ferocious brute! Oh, look at him!"

In spite of their numbers, they seemed afraid of me, seemed actually to hold me in a kind of horror—me, an animal lover, and without a gun! I felt it bitterly. "How is it," I thought, "that not one of them seems to have an inkling of what it means to be a sportsman, not one, of them seems to comprehend the instinct which makes one love sport just for the—er—danger of it?" The hare spoke again.

"Foxes," it murmured, "kill for the love of killing. Man is a kind of fox." A violent dissent at once rose from the foxes, till of one them, who seemed the eldest, said: "We certainly kill as much as we can, but we should always carry it all off and eat it if man gave us time—the ferocious brutes!" You cannot expect much of foxes, but it struck me as especially foxy that he should put the wanton character of his destructiveness off on man, especially when he must have known how carefully we preserve the fox, in the best interests of sport. A pheasant ejaculated shrilly: "He killed sixty of us one day to his own gun, and went off that same evening without eating even a wing!" And again came that shivering whisper: "Look at him! The ferocious brute! Oh, look at him!" It was too absurd! As if they could not realise that a sportsman shoots almost entirely for the mouths of others! But I checked myself, remembering that altruism is a purely human attribute. "They get a big price for us!" said a woodcock, "especially if they shoot us early. *I* fetched several shillings." Really, the ignorance of these birds! As if modern sportsmen knew anything of what happens after a day's shooting! All that is left to the butler and the keeper. Beaters, of course, and cartridges must be paid for, to say nothing of the sin of waste. "I would not think them so much worse than foxes," said a rabbit, "if they didn't often hurt you, so that you take hours dying. I was seven hours dying in great agony, and one of my brothers was twelve. Weren't you, brother?" A second rabbit nodded. "But perhaps that's better than trapping," he said. "Remember mother!" "Ah!" a partridge muttered, "foxes at all events do bite your head off clean. But men often break your wing, or your leg, and leave you!" And again that shivering whisper rose: "Look at him! The ferocious brute! Oh, look at him!"

By this time the whole thing was so getting on my nerves that if I could have risen I should have rushed at them, but a weight as of lead seemed to bind me to the ground, and all I could do was to thank God that they did not seem to know of my condition, for, though there were no man-eaters among them, I could not tell what they might do if they realised that I was helpless—the sentiments of chivalry and generosity being confined to man, as we all know.

"Yes," said the capercailzie slowly, "I am a shy bird, and was often shot at before this one got me; and though I'm strong, my size is so against me that I always took a pellet or two away with me; and what can you do then? Those ferocious brutes take the shot out of their faces and hands when they shoot each other by mistake—I've seen them; but we have no chance to do that." A snipe said shrilly: "What I object to is that he doesn't eat us till he's had too much already. I come in on toast at the fifth course; it hurts one's feelings."

"Ferocious brute, killing everything he sees."

I felt my blood fairly boil, and longed to cry out: "You beasts! You know that we don't kill everything we see! We leave that to cockneys, and foreigners." But just as I had no power of movement, so I seemed to have no power of speech. And suddenly a little voice, high up over me, piped down: "They never shoot us larks." I have always loved the lark; how grateful I felt to that little creature—till it added: "They do worse; they take and shut us up in little traps of wire till we pine away! Ferocious brutes!" In all my life I think I never was more disappointed! The second cougar spoke: "He once passed within spring of me. What do you say, friends; shall we go for him?" The shivering answer came from all: "Go for him! Ferocious brute! Oh, go for him!" And I heard the sound of hundreds of soft wings and pads ruffling and shuffling. And, knowing that I had no power to move an inch, I shut my eyes. Lying there motionless, as a beetle that shams dead, I felt them creeping, creeping, till all round me and over me was the sound of nostrils sniffing; and every second I expected to feel the nip of teeth and beaks in the fleshy parts of me. But nothing came, and with an effort I reopened my eyes. There they were, hideously close, with an expression on their faces that I could not read; a sort of wry look, every nose and beak turned a little to one side. And suddenly I heard the old fox saying: "It's impossible, with a smell like that; we could never eat him!" From every one of them came a sort of sniff or sneeze as of disgust, and as they began to back away I distinctly heard the hyena mutter: "He's not wholesome—not wholesome—the ferocious brute!"

The relief of that moment was swamped by my natural indignation that these impudent birds and beasts should presume to think that I, a British sportsman, would not be good to eat. Then that beastly hyena added: "If we killed him, you know, and buried him for a few days, he might be tolerable."

An old cock grouse called out at once: "Go back! Let us hang him! *We* are always well hung. They like us a little decayed—ferocious brutes! Go back!" And once more I felt, from the stir and shuffle, that my fate hung in the balance; and I shut my eyes again, lest they might be tempted to begin on them. Then, to my infinite relief, I heard the cougar—have we not always been told that they were the friends of man?—mutter: "Pah! It's clear we could never eat him fresh, and what we do not eat at once we do not touch!"

All the birds cried out in chorus: "No! That would be crow's work." And again I felt that I was saved. Then, to my horror, that infernal loon shrieked: "Kill him and have him stuffed—specimen of Ferocious Brute! Or fix his skin on a tree, and look at it—as he did with me!"

For a full minute I could feel the currents of opinion swaying over me, at this infamous proposal; then the old black-cock, the one whose tail is in my wife's hat, said sharply: "Specimen! He's not good enough!" And once more, for all my indignation at that gratuitous insult, I breathed freely.

"Come!" said the lady bear quietly: "Let us dribble on him a little, and go. The ferocious brute is not worth more!" And, during what seemed to me an eternity, one by one they came up, deposited on me a little saliva, looking into my eyes the while with a sort of horror and contempt, then vanished on the moor. The last to come up was the little meerkat without its head. It stood there; it could neither look at me nor drop saliva, but somehow it contrived to say: "I forgive you, ferocious brute; but I was very happy!" Then it, too, withdrew. And from all around, out of invisible presences in the air and the heather, came once more the shivering whisper: "Look at him! The ferocious brute! Oh, look at him!"

I sat up. There was a trilling sound in my ears. Above me in the blue a curlew was passing, uttering its cry. Ah! Thank Heaven!—I had been asleep! My day-dream had been caused by the potted grouse, and the pressure of the *Review*, which had lain, face downwards, on my chest, open at the page where I had been reading about the man-eating lions, and the death of those ferocious brutes. It shows what tricks of disproportion little things will play with the mind when it is not under reasonable control.

And, to get the unwholesome taste of it all out of my mouth, I at once jumped up and started for home at a round pace.

GROTESQUES

KYNHΔON

I

The Angel Æthereal, on his official visit to the Earth in 1947, paused between the Bank and the Stock Exchange to smoke a cigarette and scrutinise the passers-by.

"How they swarm," he said, "and with what seeming energy—in such an atmosphere! Of what can they be made?"

"Of money, sir," replied his dragoman; "in the past, the present, or the future. Stocks are booming. The barometer of joy stands very high. Nothing like it has been known for thirty years; not, indeed, since the days of the Great Skirmish."

"There is, then, a connection between joy and money?" remarked the Angel, letting smoke dribble through his chiselled nostrils.

"Such is the common belief; though to prove it might take time. I will, however, endeavour to do this if you desire it, sir."

"I certainly do," said the Angel; "for a less joyous-looking crowd I have seldom seen. Between every pair of brows there is a furrow, and no one whistles."

"You do not understand," returned his dragoman; "nor indeed is it surprising, for it is not so much the money as the thought that some day you need no longer make it which causes joy."

"If that day is coming to all," asked the Angel, "why do they not look joyful?"

"It is not so simple as that, sir. To the majority of these persons that day will never come, and many of them know it—these are called clerks; to some amongst the others, even, it will not come—these will be called bankrupts; to the rest it will come, and they will live at Wimblehurst and other islands of the blessed, when they have become so accustomed to making money that to cease making it will be equivalent to boredom, if not torture, or when they are so old that they can but spend it in trying to modify the disabilities of age."

"What price joy, then?" said the Angel, raising his eyebrows. "For that, I fancy, is the expression you use?"

"I perceive, sir," answered his dragoman, "that you have not yet regained your understanding of the human being, and especially of the breed which inhabits this country. Illusion is what we are after. Without our illusions we might just as well be angels or Frenchmen, who pursue at all events to some extent the sordid reality known as '*le plaisir*,' or enjoyment of life. In pursuit of illusion we go on making money and furrows in our brows, for the process is wearing. I speak, of course, of the bourgeoisie or Patriotic classes; for the practice of the Laborious is different, though their illusions are the same."

"How?" asked the Angel briefly.

"Why, sir, both hold the illusion that they will one day be joyful through the possession of money; but whereas the Patriotic expect to make it through the labour of the Laborious, the Laborious expect to make it through the labour of the Patriotic."

"Ha, ha!" said the Angel.

"Angels may laugh," replied his dragoman, "but it is a matter to make men weep."

"You know your own business best," said the Angel, "I suppose."

"Ah! sir, if we did, how pleasant it would be. It is frequently my fate to study the countenances and figures of the population, and I find the joy which the pursuit of illusion brings them is insufficient to counteract the confined, monotonous, and worried character of their lives."

"They are certainly very plain," said the Angel.

"They are," sighed his dragoman, "and getting plainer every day. Take for instance that one," and he pointed to a gentleman going up the steps. "Mark how he is built. The top of his grizzled head is narrow, the bottom of it broad. His body is short and thick and square; his legs even thicker, and his feet turn out too much; the general effect is almost pyramidal. Again, take this one," and he indicated a gentleman coming down the steps, "you could thread his legs and body through a needle's eye, but his head would defy you. Mark his boiled eyes, his flashing spectacles, and the absence of all hair. Disproportion, sir, has become endemic."

"Can this not be corrected?" asked the Angel.

"To correct a thing," answered his dragoman, "you must first be aware of it, and these are not; no more than they are aware that it is disproportionate to spend six days out of every seven in a counting-house or factory. Man, sir, is the creature of habit, and when his habits are bad, man is worse."

"I have a headache," said the Angel; "the noise is more deafening than it was when I was here in 1910."

"Yes, sir; since then we have had the Great Skirmish, an event which furiously intensified money-making. We, like every other people, have ever since been obliged to cultivate the art of getting five out of two-and-two. The progress of civilisation has been considerably speeded-up thereby, and everything but man has benefited; even horses, for they are no longer over-loaded and overdriven up Tower Hill or any other."

"How is that," asked the Angel, "if the pressure of work is greater?"

"Because they are extinct," said his dragoman; "entirely superseded by electric and air traction, as you see."

"You appear to be inimical to money," the Angel interjected, with a pen-etrating look. "Tell me, would you really rather own one shilling than five and sixpence?"

"Sir," replied his dragoman, "you are putting the candidate before the caucus, as the saying is. For money is nothing but the power to purchase what one wants. You should rather be inquiring what I want."

"Well, what do you?" said the Angel.

"To my thinking," answered his dragoman, "instead of endeavouring to increase money when we found ourselves so very bankrupt, we should have endeavoured to decrease our wants. The path of real progress, sir, is the sim-plification of life and desire till we have dispensed even with trousers and wear a single clean garment reaching to the knees; till we are content with exercising our own limbs on the solid earth; the eating of simple food we have grown ourselves; the hearing of our own voices, and tunes on oaten straws; the feel on our faces of the sun and rain and wind; the scent of the fields and woods; the homely roof, and the comely wife unspoiled by heels, pearls, and powder; the domestic animals at play, wild birds singing, and children brought up to colder water than their fathers. It should have been our business to pursue health till we no longer needed the interior of the chemist's shop, the optician's store, the hairdresser's, the corset-maker's, the thousand-and-one emporiums which patch and prink us, promoting our fan-cies and disguising the ravages which modern life makes in our figures. Our ambition should have been to need so little that, with our present scientific knowledge, we should have been able to produce it very easily and quickly, and have had abundant leisure and sound nerves and bodies wherewith to enjoy nature, art, and the domestic affections. The tragedy of man, sir, is his senseless and insatiate curiosity and greed, together with his incurable habit of neglecting the present for the sake of a future which will never come."

"You speak like a book," said the Angel.

"I wish I did," retorted his dragoman, "for no book I am able to procure enjoins us to stop this riot, and betake ourselves to the pleasurable simplicity which alone can save us."

"You would be bored stiff in a week," said the Angel.

"We should, sir," replied his dragoman, "because from our schooldays we are brought up to be acquisitive, competitive, and restless. Consider the baby in the perambulator, absorbed in contemplating the heavens and sucking its own thumb. Existence, sir, should be like that."

"A beautiful metaphor," said the Angel.

"As it is, we do but skip upon the hearse of life."

"You would appear to be of those whose motto is: 'Try never to leave things as you find them,'" observed the Angel.

"Ah, sir!" responded his dragoman, with a sad smile, "the part of a dragoman is rather ever to try and find things where he leaves them."

"Talking of that," said the Angel dreamily, "when I was here in 1910, I bought some Marconis for the rise. What are they at now?"

"I cannot tell you," replied his dragoman in a deprecating voice, "but this I will say: Inventors are not only the benefactors but the curses of mankind, and will be so long as we do not find a way of adapting their discoveries to our very limited digestive powers. The chronic dyspepsia of our civilisation, due to the attempt to swallow every pabulum which ingenuity puts before it, is so violent that I sometimes wonder whether we shall survive until your visit in 1984."

"Ah!" said the Angel, pricking his ears; "you really think there is a chance?"

"I do indeed," his dragoman answered gloomily. "Life is now one long telephone call—and what's it all about? A tour in darkness! A rattling of wheels under a sky of smoke! A never-ending game of poker!"

"Confess," said the Angel, "that you have eaten something which has not agreed with you?"

"It is so," answered his dragoman; "I have eaten of modernity, the damnedest dish that was ever set to lips. Look at those fellows," he went on, "busy as ants from nine o'clock in the morning to seven in the evening. And look at their wives!"

"Ah! yes," said the Angel cheerily; "let us look at their wives," and with three strokes of his wings he passed to Oxford Street.

"Look at them!" repeated his dragoman, "busy as ants from ten o'clock in the morning to five in the evening."

"Plain is not the word for *them*," said the Angel sadly. "What are they after, running in and out of these shop-holes?"

"Illusion, sir. The romance of business there, the romance of commerce here. They have got into these habits and, as you know, it is so much easier to get in than to get out. Would you like to see one of their homes?"

"No, no," said the Angel, starting back and coming into contact with a lady's hat. "Why do they have them so large?" he asked, with a certain irritation.

"In order that they may have them small next season," replied his dragoman. "The future, sir; the future! The cycle of beauty and eternal hope, and, incidentally, *the good of trade*. Grasp that phrase and you will have no need for further inquiry, and probably no inclination."

"One could get American sweets in here, I guess," said the Angel, entering.

II

"And where would you wish to go today, sir?" asked his dragoman of the Angel, who was moving his head from side to side like a dromedary, in the Haymarket.

"I should like," the Angel answered, "to go into the country."

"The country!" returned his dragoman, doubtfully. "You will find very little to see there."

"Natheless," said the Angel, spreading his wings.

"These," gasped his dragoman, after a few breathless minutes, "are the Chilterns—they will serve; any part of the country is now the same. Shall we descend?"

Alighting on what seemed to be a common, he removed the cloud moisture from his brow, and shading his eyes with his hand, stood peering into the distance on every side. "As I thought," he said; "there has been no movement since I brought the Prime here in 1944; we shall have some difficulty in getting lunch."

"A wonderfully peaceful spot," said the Angel.

"True," said his dragoman. "We might fly sixty miles in any direction and not see a house in repair."

"Let us!" said the Angel. They flew a hundred and alighted again.

"Same here!" said his dragoman. "This is Leicestershire. Note the rolling landscape of wild pastures."

"I am getting hungry," said the Angel. "Let us fly again."

"I have told you, sir," remarked his dragoman, while they were flying, "that we shall have the greatest difficulty in finding any inhabited dwelling in the country. Had we not better alight at Blackton or Bradleeds?"

"No," said the Angel. "I have come for a day in the fresh air."

"Would bilberries serve?" asked his dragoman; "for I see a man gathering them."

The Angel closed his wings, and they dropped on to a moor close to an aged man.

"My worthy wight," said the Angel, "we are hungry. Would you give us some of your bilberries?"

"Wot oh!" ejaculated the ancient party; "never 'eard yer comin'. Been flyin' by wireless, 'ave yer? Got an observer, I see," he added, jerking his grizzled chin at the dragoman. "Strike me, it's the good old dyes o' the Gryte Skirmish over agyne."

"Is this," asked the Angel, whose mouth was already black with bilberries, "the dialect of rural England?"

"I will interrogate him, sir," said his dragoman, "for in truth I am at a loss to account for the presence of a man in the country." He took the old person by his last button and led him a little apart. Returning to the Angel, who had finished the bilberries, he whispered:

"It is as I thought. This is the sole survivor of the soldiers settled on the land at the conclusion of the Great Skirmish. He lives on berries and birds who have died a natural death."

"I fail to understand," answered the Angel. "Where is all the rural population, where the mansions of the great, the thriving farmer, the contented peasant, the labourer about to have his minimum wage, the Old, the Merrie England of 1910?"

"That," responded his dragoman somewhat dramatically, extending his hand towards the old man, "*that* is the rural population, and he a cockney hardened in the Great Skirmish, or he could never have stayed the course."

"What!" said the Angel; "is no food grown in all this land?"

"Not a cabbage," replied his dragoman; "not a mustard and cress—outside the towns, that is."

"I perceive," said the Angel, "that I have lost touch with much that is of interest. Give me, I pray, a brief sketch of the agricultural movement."

"Why, sir," replied his dragoman, "the agricultural movement in this country since the days of the Great Skirmish, when all were talking of re-settling the land, may be summed up in two words: 'Town expansion.' In order to make this clear to you, however, I must remind you of the political currents of the past thirty years. You will not recollect that during the Great Skirmish, beneath the seeming absence of politics, there were germinating the Parties of the future. A secret but resolute intention was forming in all minds to immolate those who had played any part in politics before and during the important world-tragedy which was then being enacted, especially such as continued to hold portfolios, or persisted in asking questions in the House of Commons, as it was then called. It was not that people held them to be responsible, but nerves required soothing, and there is no anodyne, as you know, sir, equal to human sacrifice. The politician was, as one may say—'off.' No sooner, of course, was peace declared than the first real General Election was held, and it was with a certain chagrin that the old Parties found themselves in the soup. The Parties which had been forming beneath the surface swept the country: one called itself the Patriotic, and was called by its opponents the Prussian Party; the other called itself the Laborious, and was called by its opponents the Loafing Party. Their representatives were nearly all new men. In the first flush of peace, with which the human mind ever associates plenty, they came out on such an even keel that no Government could pass anything at all. Since, however, it was imperative to find the interest on a National Debt of £8,000,000,000, a further election was needed. This time, though the word Peace remained, the word Plenty had already vanished; and the Laborious Party, which, having much less to tax, felt that it could tax more freely, found itself in an overwhelming majority. You will be curious to hear, sir, of what elements this Party was composed. Its solid bulk were the returned soldiers, and the other manual workers of the country; but to this main body there was added a rump, of pundits, men of excellent intentions, brains, and principles, such as in old days had been known as Radicals and advanced Liberals. These had joined out of despair, feeling that otherwise their very existence was jeopardised. To this collocation—and to one or two other circumstances, as you will presently see, sir—the doom of the land must be traced. Now, the Laborious Party, apart from its rump, on which it would or could not sit—we shall never know now—had views about the resettlement of the land not far divergent from those held by the Patriotic Party, and they proceeded to put a scheme into operation, which, for perhaps a year, seemed to have a prospect of success. Many returned soldiers were established in favourable localities, and there was even a disposition to place the country on a self-sufficing basis in regard to food. But they had not been in power eighteen months when their rump—which, as I have told you, contained nearly all their principles—had a severe attack of these. 'Free Trade,'—which, say what you will, follows the line of least resistance and is based on the 'good of trade'—was, they perceived, endangered, and they began to agitate against bonuses on corn and preferential treatment of a pampered industry. The bonus on corn was in consequence rescinded in 1924, and in lieu thereof the system of small holdings was extended—on paper. At the same time the somewhat stunning taxation which had been placed upon the wealthy began to cause the break-up of landed estates. As the general bankruptcy and exhaustion of Europe became more and more apparent the notion of danger from future war began to seem increasingly remote, and the 'good of trade' became again the one object before every British eye. Food from overseas was cheapening once more. The inevitable occurred. Country mansions became a drug in the market, farmers farmed at a loss; small holders went bust daily, and emigrated; agricultural labourers sought the towns. In 1926 the Laborious Party, who had carried the taxation of their opponents to a pitch beyond the power of human endurance, got what the racy call 'the knock,' and the four years which followed witnessed the bitterest internecine struggle within the memory of every journalist. In the course of this strife emigration increased and the land emptied rapidly. The final victory of the Laborious Party, in 1930, saw them, still propelled by their rump, committed, among other things, to a pure town policy. They have never been out of power since; the result you see. Food is now entirely brought from overseas, largely by submarine and air service, in tabloid form, and expanded to its original proportions on arrival by an ingenious process discovered by a German. The country is now used only as a subject for sentimental poets, and to fly over, or by lovers on bicycles at weekends."

"*Mon Dieu!*" said the Angel thoughtfully: "To me, indeed, it seems that this must have been a case of: 'Oh! What a surprise!'"

"You are not mistaken, sir," replied his dragoman; "people still open their mouths over this consummation. It is pre-eminently an instance of what will happen sometimes when you are not looking, even to the English, who have been most fortunate in this respect. For you must remember that all Parties, even the Pundits, have always declared that rural life and all that, don't you know? is most necessary, and have ever asserted that they were fostering it to the utmost. But they forgot to remember that our circumstances, traditions, education, and vested interests so favoured town life and the 'good of trade' that it required a real and unparliamentary effort not to take that line of least resistance. In fact, we have here a very good example of what I told you the other day was our most striking characteristic—never knowing where we are till after the event. But what with fog and principles, how can you expect we should? Better be a little town blighter with no constitution and high political principles, than your mere healthy country product of a pampered industry. But you have not yet seen the other side of the moon."

"To what do you refer?" asked the Angel.

"Why, sir, to the glorious expansion of the towns. To this I shall introduce you tomorrow, if such be your pleasure."

"Is London, then, not a town?" asked the Angel playfully.

"London?" cried his dragoman; "a mere pleasure village. To which real town shall I take you? Liverchester?"

"Anywhere," said the Angel, "where I can get a good dinner." So saying, he paid the rural population with a smile and spread his wings.

III

"The night is yet young," said the Angel Æthereal on leaving the White Heart Hostel at Liverchester, "and I have had perhaps too much to eat. Let us walk and see the town."

"As you will, sir," replied his dragoman; "there is no difference between night and day, now that they are using the tides for the provision of electric power."

The Angel took a note of the fact. "What do they manufacture here?" he asked.

"The entire town," returned his dragoman, "which now extends from the old Liverpool to the old Manchester (as indeed its name implies), is occupied with expanding the tabloids of food which are landed in its port from the new worlds. This and the town of Brister, reaching from the old Bristol to the old Gloucester, have had the monopoly of food expansion for the United Kingdom since 1940."

"By what means precisely?" asked the Angel.

"Congenial environment and bacteriology," responded his dragoman. They walked for some time in silence, flying a little now and then in the dirtier streets, before the Angel spoke again:

"It is curious," he said, "but I perceive no difference between this town and those I remember on my visit in 1910, save that the streets are better lighted, which is not an unmixed joy, for they are dirty and full of people whose faces do not please me."

"Ah! sir," replied his dragoman, "it is too much to expect that the wonderful darkness which prevailed at the time of the Great Skirmish could endure; then, indeed, one could indulge the hope that the houses were all built by Wren, and the people all clean and beautiful. There is no poetry now."

"No!" said the Angel, sniffing, "but there is atmosphere, and it is not agreeable."

"Mankind, when herded together, *will* smell," answered his dragoman. "You cannot avoid it. What with old clothes, patchouli, petrol, fried fish and the fag, those five essentials of human life, the atmosphere of Turner and Corot are as nothing."

"But do you not run your towns to please yourselves?" said the Angel.

"Oh, no, sir! The resistance would be dreadful. They run us. You see, they are so very big, and have such prestige. Besides," he added, "even if we dared, we should not know how. For, though some great and good man once brought us plane-trees, we English are above getting the best out of life and its conditions, and despise light Frenchified taste. Notice the principle which governs this twenty-mile residential stretch. It was intended to be light, but how earnest it has all turned out! You can tell at a glance that these dwellings belong to the species 'house' and yet are individual houses, just as a man belongs to the species 'man,' and yet, as they say, has a soul of his own. This principle was introduced off the Avenue Road a few years before the Great Skirmish, and is now universal. Any person who lives in a house identical with another house is not known. Has anything heavier and more conscientious ever been seen?"

"Does this principle also apply to the houses of the working-man?" inquired the Angel.

"Hush, sir!" returned his dragoman looking round him nervously; "a dangerous word. The LABORIOUS dwell in palaces built after the design of an architect called Jerry, with communal kitchens and baths."

"Do they use them?" asked the Angel with some interest.

"Not as yet, indeed," replied his dragoman; "but I believe they are thinking of it. As you know, sir, it takes time to introduce a custom. Thirty years is but as yesterday."

"The Japanese wash daily," mused the Angel.

"Not a Christian nation," replied his dragoman; "nor have they the dirt to contend with which is conspicuous here. Let us do justice to the discouragement which dogs the ablutions of such as know they will soon be dirty again. It was confidently supposed, at the time of the Great Skirmish, which introduced military discipline and so entirely abolished caste, that the habit of washing would at last become endemic throughout the whole population. Judge how surprised were we of that day when the facts turned out otherwise. Instead of the Laborious washing more, the Patriotic washed less. It may have been the higher price of soap, or merely that human life was not very highly regarded at the time. We cannot tell. But not until military discipline disappeared, and caste was restored, which happened the moment peace returned, did the survivors of the Patriotic begin to wash immoderately again, leaving the Laborious to preserve a level more suited to democracy."

"Talking of levels," said the Angel; "is the populace increasing in stature?"

"Oh, no, indeed!" responded his dragoman; "the latest statistics give a diminution of one inch and a half during the past generation."

"And in longevity?" asked the Angel.

"As to that, babies and old people are now communally treated, and all those diseases which are curable by lymph are well in hand."

"Do people, then, not die?"

"Oh, yes, sir! About as often as before. There are new complaints which redress the balance."

"And what are those?"

"A group of diseases called for convenience Scienticitis. Some think they come from the present food system; others from the accumulation of lymphs in the body; others, again, regard them as the result of dwelling on the subject—a kind of hypnotisation by death; a fourth school hold them traceable to town air; while a fifth consider them a mere manifestation of jealousy on the part of Nature. They date, one may say with confidence, from the time of the Great Skirmish, when men's minds were turned with some anxiety to the question of statistics, and babies were at a premium."

"Is the population, then, much larger?"

"You mean smaller, sir, do you not? Not perhaps so much smaller as you might expect; but it is still nicely down. You see, the Patriotic Party, including even those Pontificals whose private practice most discouraged all that sort of thing, began at once to urge propagation. But their propaganda was, as one may say, brain-spun; and at once bumped-up—pardon the colloquialism—against the economic situation. The existing babies, it is true, were saved; the trouble was rather that the babies began not to exist. The same, of course, obtained in every European country, with the exception of what was still, in a manner of speaking, Russia; and if that country had but retained its homogeneity, it would soon by sheer numbers have swamped the rest of Europe. Fortunately, perhaps, it did not remain homogeneous. An incurable reluctance to make food for cannon and impose further burdens on selves already weighted to the ground by taxes, developed in the peoples of each Central and Western land; and in the years from 1920 to 1930 the downward curve was so alarming in Great Britain that if the Patriotic Party could only have kept office long enough at a time they would, no doubt, have enforced conception at the point of the bayonet. Luckily or unluckily, according to taste, they did not; and it was left for more natural causes to produce the inevitable reaction which began to set in after 1930, when the population of the United Kingdom had been reduced to some twenty-five millions. About that time commerce revived. The question of the land had been settled by its unconscious abandonment, and people began to see before them again the possibility of supporting families. The ingrained disposition of men and women to own pets, together with 'the good of trade,' began once more to have its way; and the population rose rapidly. A renewed joy in life, and the assurance of not having to pay the piper, caused the slums, as they used to be called, to swarm once more, and filled the communal crèches. And had it not been for the fact that any one with physical strength, or love of fresh air, promptly emigrated to the Sister Nations on attaining the age of eighteen we might now, sir, be witnessing an overcrowding equal to that of the times before the Great Skirmish. The movement is receiving an added impetus with the approach of the Greater Skirmish between the Teutons and Mongolians, for it is expected that trade will boom and much wealth accrue to those countries which are privileged to look on with equanimity at this great new drama, as the editors are already calling it."

"In all this," said the Angel Æthereal, "I perceive something rather sordid."

"Sir," replied his dragoman earnestly, "your remark is characteristic of the sky, where people are not made of flesh and blood; pay, I believe, no taxes; and have no experience of the devastating consequences of war. I recollect so well when I was a young man, before the Great Skirmish began, and even when it had been going on several years, how glibly the leaders of opinion talked of human progress, and how blind they were to the fact that it has a certain connection with environment. You must remember that ever since that large and, as some still think rather tragic, occurrence environment has been very dicky and Utopia not unrelated to thin air. It has been perceived time and again that the leaders of public opinion are not always confirmed by events. The new world, which was so sapiently prophesied by rhetoricians, is now nigh thirty years old, and, for my part, I confess to surprise that it is not worse than it actually is. I am moralising, I fear, however, for these suburban buildings grievously encourage the philosophic habit. Rather let us barge along and see the Laborious at their labours, which are never interrupted now by the mere accident of night."

The Angel increased his speed till they alighted amid a forest of tall chimneys, whose sirens were singing like a watch of nightingales.

"There is a shift on," said the dragoman. "Stand here, sir; we shall see them passing in and out."

The Laborious were not hurrying, and went by uttering the words: "Cheer oh!" "So long!" and "Wot abaht it!"

The Angel contemplated them for a time before he said: "It comes back to me now how they used to talk when they were doing up my flat on my visit in 1910."

"Give me, I pray, an imitation," said his dragoman.

The Angel struck the attitude of one painting a door. "William," he said, rendering those voices of the past, "what money are you obtaining?"

"Not half, Alfred."

"If that is so, indeed, William, should you not rather leave your tools and obtain better money? I myself am doing this."

"Not half, Alfred."

"Round the corner I can obtain more money by working for fewer hours. In my opinion there is no use in working for less money when you can obtain more. How much does Henry obtain?"

"Not half, Alfred."

"What I am now obtaining is, in my opinion, no use at all."

"Not half, Alfred."

Here the Angel paused, and let his hand move for one second in a masterly exhibition of activity.

"It is doubtful, sir," said his dragoman, "whether you would be permitted to dilute your conversation with so much labour in these days; the rules are very strict."

"Are there, then, still Trades Unions?" asked the Angel.

"No, indeed," replied his dragoman; "but there are Committees. That habit which grew up at the time of the Great Skirmish has flourished ever since. Statistics reveal the fact that there are practically no adults in the country between the ages of nineteen and fifty who are not sitting on Committees. At the time of the Great Skirmish all Committees were nominally active; they are now both active and passive. In every industry, enterprise, or walk of life a small active Committee directs; and a large passive Committee, formed of everybody else, resists that direction. And it is safe to say that the Passive Committees are active and the Active Committees passive; in this way no inordinate amount of work is done. Indeed, if the tongue and the electric button had not usurped practically all the functions of the human hand, the State would have some difficulty in getting its boots blacked. But a ha'poth of visualisation is worth three lectures at ten shillings the stall, so enter, sir, and see for yourself."

Saying this, he pushed open the door.

In a shed, which extended beyond the illimitable range of the Angel's eye, machinery and tongues were engaged in a contest which filled the ozone with an incomparable hum. Men and women in profusion were leaning against walls or the pillars on which the great roof was supported, assiduously pressing buttons. The scent of expanding food revived the Angel's appetite.

"I shall require supper," he said dreamily.

"By all means, sir," replied his dragoman; "after work—play. It will afford you an opportunity to witness modern pleasures in our great industrial centres. But what a blessing is electric power!" he added. "Consider these lilies of the town, they toil not, neither do they spin——"

"Yet Solomon in all his glory," chipped in the Angel eagerly, "had not their appearance, you bet."

"Indeed they are an insouciant crowd," mused his dragoman; "How tinkling is their laughter! The habit dates from the days of the Great Skirmish, when nothing but laughter would meet the case."

"Tell me," said the Angel, "are the English satisfied at last with their industrial conditions, and generally with their mode of life in these expanded towns?"

"Satisfied? Oh dear, no, sir! But you know what it is: They are obliged to wait for each fresh development before they can see what they have to counteract; and, since that great creative force, 'the good of trade,' is always a little stronger than the forces of criticism and reform, each development carries them a little further on the road to——"

"Hell! How hungry I am again!" exclaimed the Angel. "Let us sup!"

IV

"Laughter," said the Angel Æthereal, applying his wineglass to his nose, "has ever distinguished mankind from all other animals with the exception of the dog. And the power of laughing at nothing distinguishes man even from that quadruped."

"I would go further, sir," returned his dragoman, "and say that the power of laughing at that which should make him sick distinguishes the Englishman from all other varieties of man except the negro. Kindly observe!" He rose, and taking the Angel by the waist, fox-trotted him among the little tables.

"See!" he said, indicating the other supper-takers with a circular movement of his beard, "they are consumed with laughter. The habit of fox-trotting in the intervals of eating has been known ever since it was introduced by Americans a generation ago, at the beginning of the Great Skirmish, when that important people had as yet nothing else to do; but it still causes laughter in this country. A distressing custom," he wheezed, as they resumed their seats, "for not only does it disturb the oyster, but it compels one to think lightly of the human species. Not that one requires much compulsion," he added, "now that music-hall, cinema, and restaurant are conjoined. What a happy idea it was of Berlin's, and how excellent for business! Kindly glance for a moment—but not more—at the left-hand stage."

The Angel turned his eyes towards a cinematograph film which was being displayed. He contemplated it for the moment without speaking.

"I do not comprehend," he said at last, "why the person with the arrested moustaches is hitting so many people with that sack of flour."

"To cause amusement, sir," replied his dragoman. "Look at the laughing faces around you."

"But it is not funny," said the Angel.

"No, indeed," returned his dragoman. "Be so good as to carry your eyes now to the stage on the right, but not for long. What do you see?"

"I see a very red-nosed man beating a very white-nosed man about the body."

"It is a real scream, is it not?"

"No," said the Angel drily. "Does nothing else ever happen on these stages?"

"Nothing. Stay! *Revues* happen!"

"What are *revues*?" asked the Angel.

"Criticisms of life, sir, as it would be seen by persons inebriated on various intoxicants."

"They should be joyous."

"They are accounted so," his dragoman replied; "but for my part, I prefer to criticise life for myself, especially when I am drunk."

"Are there no plays, no operas?" asked the Angel from behind his glass.

"Not in the old and proper sense of these words. They disappeared towards the end of the Great Skirmish."

"What food for the mind is there, then?" asked the Angel, adding an oyster to his collection.

"None in public, sir, for it is well recognised, and has been ever since those days, that laughter alone promotes business and removes the thought of death. You cannot recall, as I can, sir, the continual stream which used to issue from theatres, music-halls, and picture-palaces in the days of the Great Skirmish, nor the joviality of the Strand and the more expensive restaurants. I have often thought," he added with a touch of philosophy, "what a height of civilisation we must have reached to go jesting, as we did, to the Great Unknown."

"Is that really what the English did at the time of the Great Skirmish?" asked the Angel.

"It is," replied his dragoman solemnly.

"Then they are a very fine people, and I can put up with much about them which seems to me distressing."

"Ah! sir, though, being an Englishman, I am sometimes inclined to disparage the English, I am yet convinced that you could not fly a week's journey and come across another race with such a peculiar nobility, or such an unconquerable soul, if you will forgive my using a word whose meaning is much disputed. May I tempt you with a clam?" he added more lightly. "We now have them from America—in fair preservation, and very nasty they are, in my opinion."

The Angel took a clam.

"My Lord!" he said, after a moment of deglutition.

"Quite so!" replied his dragoman. "But kindly glance at the right-hand stage again. There is a *revue* on now. What do you see?"

The Angel made two holes with his forefingers and thumbs and, putting them to his eyes, bent a little forward.

"Tut, tut!" he said; "I see some attractive young females with very few clothes on, walking up and down in front of what seem to me, indeed, to be two grownup men in collars and jackets as of little boys. What precise criticism of life is this conveying?"

His dragoman answered in reproachful accents:

"Do you not feel, sir, from your own sensations, how marvellously this informs one of the secret passions of mankind? Is there not in it a striking revelation of the natural tendencies of the male population? Remark how the whole audience, including your august self, is leaning forward and looking through their thumb-holes?"

The Angel sat back hurriedly.

"True," he said, "I was carried away. But that is not the criticism of life which art demands. If it had been, the audience, myself included, would have been sitting back with their lips curled dry, instead of watering."

"For all that," replied his dragoman, "it is the best we can give you; anything which induces the detached mood of which you spoke, has been banned from the stage since the days of the Great Skirmish; it is so very bad for business."

"Pity!" said the Angel, imperceptibly edging forward; "the mission of art is to elevate."

"It is plain, sir," said his dragoman, "that you have lost touch with the world as it is. The mission of art—now truly democratic—is to level—in principle up, in practice down. Do not forget, sir, that the English have ever regarded æstheticism as unmanly, and grace as immoral; when to that basic principle you add the principle of serving the taste of the majority, you have perfect conditions for a sure and gradual decrescendo."

"Does taste, then, no longer exist?" asked the Angel.

"It is not wholly, as yet, extinct, but lingers in the communal kitchens and canteens, as introduced by the Young Men's Christian Association in the days of the Great Skirmish. While there is appetite there is hope, nor is it wholly discouraging that taste should now centre in the stomach; for is not that the real centre of man's activity? Who dare affirm that from so universal a foundation the fair structure of æstheticism shall not be rebuilt? The eye, accustomed to the look of dainty dishes and pleasant cookery, may once more demand the architecture of Wren, the sculpture of Rodin, the paintings of— dear me—whom? Why, sir, even before the days of the Great Skirmish, when you were last on earth, we had already begun to put the future of æstheticism on a more real basis, and were converting the concert-halls of London into hotels. Few at the time saw the far-reaching significance of that movement, or realised that æstheticism was to be levelled down to the stomach, in order that it might be levelled up again to the head, on true democratic principles."

"But what," said the Angel, with one of his preternatural flashes of acumen, "what if, on the other hand, taste should continue to sink and lose even its present hold on the stomach? If all else has gone, why should not the beauty of the kitchen go?"

"That indeed," sighed his dragoman, placing his hand on his heart, "is a thought which often gives me a sinking sensation. Two liqueur brandies," he murmured to the waiter. "But the stout heart refuses to despair. Besides, advertisements show decided traces of æsthetic advance. All the great painters, poets, and fiction writers are working on them; the movement had its origin in the propaganda demanded by the Great Skirmish. You will not recollect the war poetry of that period, the patriotic films, the death cartoons, and other remarkable achievements. We have just as great talents now, though their object has not perhaps the religious singleness of those stirring times. Not a food, corset, or collar which has not its artist working for it! Toothbrushes, nut-crackers, babies' baths—the whole caboodle of manufacture—are now set to music. Such themes are considered subliminal if not sublime. No, sir, I will not despair; it is only at moments when I have dined poorly that the horizon seems dark. Listen—they have turned on the 'Kalophone,' for you must know that all music now is beautifully made by machine—so much easier for every one."

The Angel raised his head, and into his eyes came the glow associated with celestial strains.

"The tune," he said, "is familiar to me."

"Yes, sir," answered his dragoman, "for it is *The Messiah* in ragtime. No time is wasted, you notice; all, even pleasure, is intensively cultivated, on the lines of least resistance, thanks to the feverishness engendered in us by the Great Skirmish, when no one knew if he would have another chance, and to the subsequent need for fostering industry. But whether we really enjoy ourselves is perhaps a question to answer which you must examine the English character."

"That I refuse to do," said the Angel.

"And you are wise, sir, for it is a puzzler, and many have cracked their heads over it. But have we not been here long enough? We can pursue our researches into the higher realms of art tomorrow."

A beam from the Angel's lustrous eyes fell on a lady at the next table. "Yes, perhaps we had better go," he sighed.

V

"And so it is through the fields of true art that we shall walk this morning?" said the Angel Æthereal.

"Such as they are in this year of Peace 1947," responded his dragoman, arresting him before a statue; "for the development of this hobby has been peculiar since you were here in 1910, when the childlike and contortionist movement was just beginning to take hold of the British."

"Whom does this represent?" asked the Angel.

"A celebrated publicist, recently deceased at a great age. You see him unfolded by this work of multiform genius, in every aspect known to art, religion, nature, and the population. From his knees downwards he is clearly devoted to nature, and is portrayed as about to enter his bath. From his waist to his knees he is devoted to religion—mark the complete disappearance of the human aspect. From his neck to his waist he is devoted to public affairs; observe the tweed coat, the watch-chain, and other signs of practical sobriety. But the head is, after all, the crown of the human being, and is devoted to art. This is why you cannot make out that it is a head. Note its pyramidal severity, its cunning little ears, its box-built, water-tightal structure. The hair you note to be in flames. Here we have the touch of beauty—the burning shrub.

In the whole you will observe that aversion from natural form and the single point of view, characteristic of all twentieth-century æsthetics. The whole thing is a very great masterpiece of childlike contortionism. To do things as irresponsibly as children and contortionists—what a happy discovery of the line of least resistance in art that was! Mark, by the way, this exquisite touch about the left hand."

"It appears to be deformed," said the Angel, going a step nearer.

"Look closer still," returned his dragoman, "and you will see that it is holding a novel of the great Russian, upside down. Ever since that simple master who so happily blended the childlike with the contortionist became known in this country they have been trying to go him one better, in letters, in painting, in sculpture, and in music, refusing to admit that he was the last cry; and until they have beaten him this movement simply cannot cease; it may therefore go on for ever, for he was the limit. That hand symbolises the whole movement."

"How?" said the Angel.

"Why, sir, somersault is its mainspring. Did you never observe the great Russian's method? Prepare your characters to do one thing, and make them very swiftly do the opposite. Thus did that terrific novelist demonstrate his overmastering range of vision and knowledge of the depths of human nature. Since his characters never varied this routine in the course of some eight thousand pages, people have lightly said that he repeated himself. But what of that? Consider what perfect dissociation he thereby attained between character and action; what nebulosity of fact; what a truly childlike and mystic mix-up of all human values hitherto known! And here, sir, at the risk of tickling you, I must whisper." The dragoman made a trumpet of his hand: "Fiction can only be written by those who have exceptionally little knowledge of ordinary human nature, and great fiction only by such as have none at all."

"How is that?" said the Angel, somewhat disconcerted.

"Surprise, sir, is the very kernel of all effects in art, and in real life people *will* act as their characters and temperaments determine that they shall. This dreadful and unmalleable trait would have upset all the great mystic masters from generation to generation if they had only noticed it. But did they? Fortunately not. These greater men naturally put into their books the greater confusion and flux in which their extraordinary selves exist! The nature they portray is not human, but super- or subter-human, which you will. Who would have it otherwise?"

"Not I," said the Angel. "For I confess to a liking for what is called the 'tuppence coloured.' But Russians are not as other men, are they?"

"They are not," said his dragoman, "but the trouble is, sir, that since the British discovered him, every character in our greater fiction has a Russian soul, though living in Cornwall or the Midlands, in a British body under a Scottish or English name."

"Very piquant," said the Angel, turning from the masterpiece before him. "Are there no undraped statues to be seen?"

"In no recognisable form. For, not being educated to the detached contemplation which still prevailed to a limited extent even as late as the days of the Great Skirmish, the populace can no longer be trusted with such works of art; they are liable to rush at them, for embrace, or demolition, as their temperaments may dictate."

"The Greeks are dead, then," said the Angel.

"As door-nails, sir. They regarded life as a thing to be enjoyed—a vice you will not have noticed in the British. The Greeks were an outdoor people, who lived in the sun and the fresh air, and had none of the niceness bred by the life of our towns. We have long been renowned for our delicacy about the body; nor has the tendency been decreased by constituting Watch Committees of young persons in every borough. These are now the arbiters of art, and nothing unsuitable to the child of seven passes their censorship."

"How careful!" said the Angel.

"The result has been wonderful," remarked his dragoman. "Wonderful!" he repeated, dreamily. "I suppose there is more smouldering sexual desire and disease in this country than in any other."

"Was that the intention?" asked the Angel.

"Oh! no, sir! That is but the natural effect of so remarkably pure a surface. All is within instead of without. Nature has now wholly disappeared. The process was sped-up by the Great Skirmish. For, since then, we have had little leisure and income to spare on the gratification of anything but laughter; this and the 'unco guid' have made our art-surface glare in the eyes of the nations, thin and spotless as if made of tin."

The Angel raised his eyebrows. "I had hoped for better things," he said.

"You must not suppose, sir," pursued his dragoman, "that there is not plenty of the undraped, so long as it is vulgar, as you saw just now upon the stage, for that is good business; the line is only drawn at the danger-point of art, which is always very bad business in this country. Yet even in real life the undraped has to be grotesque to be admitted; the one fatal quality is natural beauty. The laugh, sir, the laugh—even the most hideous and vulgar laugh— is such a disinfectant. I should, however, say in justice to our literary men, that they have not altogether succumbed to the demand for cachinnations. A school, which first drew breath before the Great Skirmish began, has perfected itself, till now we have whole tomes where hardly a sentence would be intelligible to any save the initiate; this enables them to defy the Watch Committees, with other Philistines. We have writers who mysteriously preach the realisation of self by never considering anybody else; of purity through experience of exotic vice; of courage through habitual cowardice; and of kindness through Prussian behaviour. They are generally young. We have others whose fiction consists of autobiography interspersed with philosophic and political fluencies. These may be of any age from eighty odd to the bitter thirties. We have also the copious and chatty novelist; and transcribers of the life of the Laborious, whom the Laborious never read. Above all, we have the great Patriotic school, who put the national motto first, and write purely what is good for trade. In fact, we have every sort, as in the old days."

"It would appear," said the Angel, "that the arts have stood somewhat still."

"Except for a more external purity, and a higher internal corruption," replied his dragoman.

"Are artists still noted for their jealousies?" asked the Angel.

"They are, sir; for that is inherent in the artistic temperament, which is extremely touchy about fame."

"And do they still get angry when those gentlemen—the——"

"Critics," his dragoman suggested. "They get angry, sir; but critics are usually anonymous, and from excellent reasons; for not only are the passions of an angry artist very high, but the knowledge of an angry critic is not infrequently very low, especially of art. It is kinder to save life, where possible."

"For my part," said the Angel, "I have little regard for human life, and consider that many persons would be better buried."

"That may be," his dragoman retorted with some irritation; "'*errare est humanum*.' But I, for one, would rather be a dead human being any day than a live angel, for I think they are more charitable."

"Well," said the Angel genially, "you have the prejudice of your kind. Have you an artist about the place, to show me? I do not recollect any at Madame Tussaud's."

"They have taken to declining that honour. We could see one in real life if we went to Cornwall."

"Why Cornwall?"

"I cannot tell you, sir. There is something in the air which affects their passions."

"I am hungry, and would rather go to the Savoy," said the Angel, walking on.

"You are in luck," whispered his dragoman, when they had seated themselves at a table covered with prawns; "for at the next on your left is our most famous exponent of the mosaic school of novelism."

"Then here goes!" replied the Angel. And, turning to his neighbour, he asked pleasantly: "How do you do, sir? What is your income?"

The gentleman addressed looked up from his prawn, and replied wearily: "Ask my agent. He may conceivably possess the knowledge you require."

"Answer me this, at all events," said the Angel, with more dignity, if possible: "How do you write your books? For it must be wonderful to summon around you every day the creatures of your imagination. Do you wait for afflatus?"

"No," said the author; "er—no! I—er——" he added weightily, "sit down every morning."

The Angel rolled his eyes and, turning to his dragoman, said in a well-bred whisper: "He sits down every morning! My Lord, how good for trade!"

VI

"A glass of sherry, dry, and ham sandwich, stale, can be obtained here, sir," said the dragoman; "and for dessert, the scent of parchment and bananas. We will then attend Court 45, where I shall show you how fundamentally our legal procedure has changed in the generation that has elapsed since the days of the Great Skirmish."

"Can it really be that the Law has changed? I had thought it immutable," said the Angel, causing his teeth to meet with difficulty: "What will be the nature of the suit to which we shall listen?"

"I have thought it best, sir, to select a divorce case, lest you should sleep, overcome by the ozone and eloquence in these places."

"Ah!" said the Angel: "I am ready."

The Court was crowded, and they took their seats with difficulty, and a lady sitting on the Angel's left wing.

"The public *will* frequent this class of case," whispered his dragoman. "How different when you were here in 1910!"

The Angel collected himself: "Tell me," he murmured, "which of the grey-haired ones is the judge?"

"He in the bag-wig, sir," returned his dragoman; "and that little lot is the jury," he added, indicating twelve gentlemen seated in two rows.

"What is their private life?" asked the Angel.

"No better than it should be, perhaps," responded his dragoman facetiously; "but no one can tell that from their words and manner, as you will presently see. These are special ones," he added, "and pay income tax, so that their judgment in matters of morality is of considerable value."

"They have wise faces," said the Angel. "Which is the prosecutor?"

"No, no!" his dragoman answered, vividly: "This is a civil case. That is the plaintiff with a little mourning about her eyes and a touch of red about her lips, in the black hat with the aigrette, the pearls, and the fashionably sober clothes."

"I see her," said the Angel: "an attractive woman. Will she win?"

"We do not call it winning, sir; for this, as you must know, is a sad matter, and implies the breaking-up of a home. She will most unwillingly receive a decree, at least, I think so," he added; "though whether it will stand the scrutiny of the King's Proctor we may wonder a little, from her appearance."

"King's Proctor?" said the Angel. "What is that?"

"A celestial Die-hard, sir, paid to join together again those whom man have put asunder."

"I do not follow," said the Angel fretfully.

"I perceive," whispered his dragoman, "that I must make clear to you the spirit which animates our justice in these matters. You know, of course, that the intention of our law is ever to penalise the wrongdoer. It therefore requires the innocent party, like that lady there, to be exceptionally innocent, not only before she secures her divorce, but for six months afterwards."

"Oh!" said the Angel. "And where is the guilty party?"

"Probably in the south of France," returned his dragoman, "with the new partner of his affections. They have a place in the sun; this one a place in the Law Courts."

"Dear me!" said the Angel. "Does she prefer that?"

"There are ladies," his dragoman replied, "who find it a pleasure to appear, no matter where, so long as people can see them in a pretty hat. But the great majority would rather sink into the earth than do this thing."

"The face of this one is most agreeable to me; I should not wish her to sink," said the Angel warmly.

"Agreeable or not," resumed his dragoman, "they have to bring their hearts for inspection by the public if they wish to become free from the party who has done them wrong. This is necessary, for the penalisation of the wrongdoer."

"And how will he be penalised?" asked the Angel naïvely.

"By receiving his freedom," returned his dragoman, "together with the power to enjoy himself with his new partner, in the sun, until in due course, he is able to marry her."

"This is mysterious to me," murmured the Angel. "Is not the boot on the wrong leg?"

"Oh! sir, the law would not make a mistake like that. You are bringing a single mind to the consideration of this matter, but that will never do. This lady is a true and much-wronged wife; that is—let us hope so!—to whom our law has given its protection and remedy; but she is also, in its eyes, somewhat reprehensible for desiring to avail herself of that protection and remedy. For, though the law is now purely the affair of the State and has nothing to do with the Appointed, it still secretly believes in the religious maxim: 'Once married, always married,' and feels that however much a married person is neglected or ill-treated, she should not desire to be free."

"She?" said the Angel. "Does a man never desire to be free?"

"Oh, yes! sir, and not infrequently."

"Does the law, then, not consider him reprehensible in that desire?"

"In theory, perhaps; but there is a subtle distinction. For, sir, as you observe from the countenances before you, the law is administered entirely by males, and males cannot but believe in the divine right of males to have a better time than females; and, though they do not say so, they naturally feel that a husband wronged by a wife is more injured than a wife wronged by a husband."

"There is much in that," said the Angel. "But tell me how the oracle is worked—for it may come in handy!"

"You allude, sir, to the necessary procedure? I will make this clear. There are two kinds of cases: what I may call the 'O.K.' and what I may call the 'rig.' Now in the 'O.K.' it is only necessary for the plaintiff, if it be a woman, to receive a black eye from her husband and to pay detectives to find out that he has been too closely in the company of another; if it be a man, he need not receive a black eye from his wife, and has merely to pay the detectives to obtain the same necessary information."

"Why this difference between the sexes?" asked the Angel.

"Because," answered his dragoman, "woman is the weaker sex, things are therefore harder for her."

"But," said the Angel, "the English have a reputation for chivalry."

"They have, sir."

"Well——" began the Angel.

"When these conditions are complied with," interrupted his dragoman, "a suit for divorce may be brought, which may or may not be defended. Now, the 'rig,' which is always brought by the wife, is not so simple, for it must be subdivided into two sections: 'Ye straight rig' and 'Ye crooked rig.' 'Ye straight rig' is where the wife cannot induce her husband to remain with her, and discovering from him that he has been in the close company of another, wishes to be free of him. She therefore tells the Court that she wishes him to come back to her, and the Court will tell him to go back. Whereupon, if he obey, the fat is sometimes in the fire. If, however, he obeys not, which is the more probable, she may, after a short delay, bring a suit, adducing the evidence she has obtained, and receive a decree. This may be the case before you, or, on the other hand, it may not, and will then be what is called 'Ye crooked rig.' If that is so, these two persons, having found that they cannot live in conjugal friendliness, have laid their heads together for the last time, and arranged to part; the procedure will now be the same as in 'Ye straight rig.' But the wife must take the greatest care to lead the Court to suppose that she really wishes her husband to come back; for, if she does not, it is collusion. The more ardent her desire to part from him, the more care she must take to pretend the opposite! But this sort of case is, after all, the simplest, for both parties are in complete accord in desiring to be free of each other, so neither does anything to retard that end, which is soon obtained."

"About that evidence?" said the Angel. "What must the man do?"

"He will require to go to an hotel with a lady friend," replied his drago-man; "once will be enough. And, provided they are called in the morning, there is no real necessity for anything else."

"H'm!" said the Angel. "This, indeed, seems to me to be all around about the bush. Could there not be some simple method which would not neces-sitate the perversion of the truth?"

"Ah, no!" responded his dragoman. "You forget what I told you, sir. However unhappy people may be together, our law grudges their separation; it requires them therefore to be immoral, or to lie, or both, before they can part."

"Curious!" said the Angel.

"You must understand, sir, that when a man says he will take a woman, and a woman says she will take a man, for the rest of their natural existence, they are assumed to know all about each other, though not permitted, of course, by the laws of morality to know anything of real importance. Since it is almost impossible from a modest acquaintanceship to make sure whether they will continue to desire each other's company after a completed knowl-edge, they are naturally disposed to go it 'blind,' if I may be pardoned the expression, and will take each other for ever on the smallest provocations. For the human being, sir, makes nothing of the words 'for ever,' when it sees immediate happiness before it. You can well understand, therefore, how nec-essary it is to make it very hard for them to get untied again."

"I should dislike living with a wife if I were tired of her," said the Angel.

"Sir," returned his dragoman confidentially, "in that sentiment you would have with you the whole male population. And, I believe, the whole of the female population would feel the same if they were tired of you, as the hus-band."

"That!" said the Angel, with a quiet smile.

"Ah! yes, sir; but does not this convince you of the necessity to force people who are tired of each other to go on living together?"

"No," said the Angel, with appalling frankness.

"Well," his dragoman replied soberly, "I must admit that some have thought our marriage laws should be in a museum, for they are unique; and, though a source of amusement to the public, and emolument to the profes-sion, they pass the comprehension of men and angels who have not the key of the mystery."

"What key?" asked the Angel.

"I will give it you, sir," said his dragoman: "The English have a genius for taking the shadow of a thing for its substance. 'So long,' they say, 'as our marriages, our virtue, our honesty, and happiness *seem* to be, they *are*.' So long, therefore, as we do not dissolve a marriage it remains virtuous, honest and happy, though the parties to it may be unfaithful, untruthful, and in misery. It would be regarded as awful, sir, for marriage to depend on mutual liking. We English cannot bear the thought of defeat. To dissolve an unhappy marriage is to recognise defeat by life, and we would rather that other people lived in wretchedness all their days than admit that members of our race had come up against something too hard to overcome. The English do not care about making the best out of this life in reality so long as they can do it in appearance."

"Then they believe in a future life?"

"They did to some considerable extent up to the 'eighties of the last century, and their laws and customs were no doubt settled in accordance therewith, and have not yet had time to adapt themselves. We are a somewhat slow-moving people, always a generation or two behind our real beliefs."

"They have lost their belief, then?"

"It is difficult to arrive at figures, sir, on such a question. But it has been estimated that perhaps one in ten adults now has some semblance of what may be called active belief in a future existence."

"And the rest are prepared to let their lives be arranged in accordance with the belief of that tenth?" asked the Angel, surprised. "Tell me, do they think their matrimonial differences will be adjusted over there, or what?"

"As to that, all is cloudy; and certain matters would be difficult to adjust without bigamy; for general opinion and the law permit the remarriage of persons whose first has gone before."

"How about children?" said the Angel; "for that is no inconsiderable item, I imagine."

"Yes, sir, they are a difficulty. But here, again, my key will fit. So long as the marriage *seems* real, it does not matter that the children know it isn't and suffer from the disharmony of their parents."

"I think," said the Angel acutely, "there must be some more earthly reason for the condition of your marriage laws than those you give me. It's all a matter of property at bottom, I suspect."

"Sir," said his dragoman, seemingly much struck, "I should not be surprised if you were right. There is little interest in divorce where no money is involved, and our poor are considered able to do without it. But I will never admit that this is the reason for the state of our divorce laws. No, no; I am an Englishman."

"Well," said the Angel, "we are wandering. Does this judge believe what they are now saying to him?"

"It is impossible to inform you, for judges are very deep and know all that is to be known on these matters. But of this you may be certain: if anything is fishy to the average apprehension, he will not suffer it to pass his nose."

"Where is the average apprehension?" asked the Angel.

"There, sir," said his dragoman, pointing to the jury with his chin, "noted for their common sense."

"And these others with grey heads who are calling each other friend, though they appear to be inimical?"

"Little can be hid from them," returned his dragoman; "but this case, though defended as to certain matters of money, is not disputed in regard to the divorce itself. Moreover, they are bound by professional etiquette to serve their clients through thin and thick."

"Cease!" said the Angel; "I wish to hear this evidence, and so does the lady on my left wing."

His dragoman smiled in his beard, and made no answer.

"Tell me," remarked the Angel, when he had listened, "does this woman get anything for saying she called them in the morning?"

"Fie, sir!" responded his dragoman; "only her expenses to the Court and back. Though indeed, it is possible that after she had called them, she got half a sovereign from the defendant to impress the matter on her mind, seeing that she calls many people every day."

"The whole matter," said the Angel, with a frown, "appears to be in the nature of a game; nor are the details as savoury as I expected."

"It would be otherwise if the case were defended, sir," returned his dragoman; "then, too, you would have had an opportunity of understanding the capacity of the human mind for seeing the same incident to be both black and white; but it would take much of your valuable time, and the Court would be so crowded that you would have a lady sitting on your right wing also, and possibly on your knee. For, as you observe, ladies are particularly attached to these dramas of real life."

"If my wife were a wrong one," said the Angel, "I suppose that, according to your law, I could not sew her up in a sack and place it in the water?"

"We are not now in the days of the Great Skirmish," replied his dragoman somewhat coldly. "At that time any soldier who found his wife unfaithful, as we call it, could shoot her with impunity and receive the plaudits and possibly a presentation from the populace, though he himself may not have been impeccable while away—a masterly method of securing a divorce. But, as I told you, our procedure has changed since then; and even soldiers now have to go to work in this roundabout fashion."

"Can he not shoot the paramour?" asked the Angel.

"Not even that," answered his dragoman. "So soft and degenerate are the days. Though, if he can invent for the paramour a German name, he will still receive but a nominal sentence. Our law is renowned for never being swayed by sentimental reasons. I well recollect a case in the days of the Great Skirmish, when a jury found contrary to the plainest facts sooner than allow that reputation for impartiality to be tarnished."

"Ah!" said the Angel absently; "what is happening now?"

"The jury are considering their verdict. The conclusion is, however, foregone, for they are not retiring. The plaintiff is now using her smelling salts."

"She is a fine woman," said the Angel emphatically.

"Hush, sir! The judge might hear you."

"What if he does?" asked the Angel in surprise.

"He would then eject you for contempt of Court."

"Does he not think her a fine woman, too?"

"For the love of justice, sir, be silent," entreated his dragoman. "This concerns the happiness of three, if not of five, lives. Look! She is lifting her veil; she is going to use her handkerchief."

"I cannot bear to see a woman cry," said the Angel, trying to rise; "please take this lady off my left wing."

"Kindly sit tight!" murmured his dragoman to the lady, leaning across behind the Angel's back. "Listen, sir!" he added to the Angel: "The jury are satisfied that what is necessary has taken place. All is well; she will get her decree."

"Hurrah!" said the Angel in a loud voice.

"If that noise is repeated, I will have the Court cleared."

"I am going to repeat it," said the Angel firmly; "she is beautiful!"

His dragoman placed a hand respectfully over the Angel's mouth. "Oh, sir!" he said soothingly, "do not spoil this charming moment. Hark! He is giving her a decree *nisi*, with costs. Tomorrow it will be in all the papers, for it helps to sell them. See! She is withdrawing; we can now go." And he disengaged the Angel's wing.

The Angel rose quickly and made his way towards the door. "I am going to walk out with her," he announced joyously.

"I beseech you," said his dragoman, hurrying beside him, "remember the King's Proctor! Where is your chivalry? For *he* has none, sir—not a little bit!"

"Bring him to me; I will give it him!" said the Angel, kissing the tips of his fingers to the plaintiff, who was vanishing in the gloom of the fresh air.

VII

In the Strangers' room of the Strangers' Club the usual solitude was reigning when the Angel Æthereal entered.

"You will be quiet here," said his dragoman, drawing up two leather chairs to the hearth, "and comfortable," he added, as the Angel crossed his legs. "After our recent experience, I thought it better to bring you where your mind would be composed, since we have to consider so important a subject as morality. There is no place, indeed, where we could be so completely sheltered from life, or so free to evolve from our inner consciousness the momentous conclusions of the armchair moralist. When you have had your sneeze," he added, glancing at the Angel, who was taking snuff, "I shall make known to you the conclusions I have formed in the course of a chequered career."

"Before you do that," said the Angel, "it would perhaps be as well to limit the sphere of our inquiry."

"As to that," remarked his dragoman, "I shall confine my information to the morals of the English since the opening of the Great Skirmish, in 1914, just a short generation of three and thirty years ago; and you will find my theme readily falls, sir, into the two main compartments of public and private morality. When I have finished you can ask me any questions."

"Proceed!" said the Angel, letting his eyelids droop.

"Public morality," his dragoman began, "is either superlative, comparative, positive, or negative. And superlative morality is found, of course, only in the newspapers. It is the special prerogative of leader writers. Its note, remote and unchallengeable, was well struck by almost every organ at the commencement of the Great Skirmish, and may be summed up in a single solemn phrase: 'We will sacrifice on the altar of duty the last life and the last dollar—except the last life and dollar of the last leader-writer.' For, as all must see, that one had to be preserved, to ensure and comment on the consummation of the sacrifice. What loftier morality can be conceived? And it has ever been a grief to the multitude that the lives of those patriots and benefactors of their species should, through modesty, have been unrevealed to such as pant to copy them. Here and there the lineaments of a tip-topper were discernible beneath the disguise of custom; but what fair existences were screened! I may tell you at once, sir, that the State was so much struck at the time of the Great Skirmish by this doctrine of the utter sacrifice of others that it almost immediately adopted the idea, and has struggled to retain it ever since. Indeed, only the unaccountable reluctance of 'others' to be utterly sacrificed has ensured their perpetuity."

"In 1910," said the Angel, "I happened to notice that the Prussians had already perfected that system. Yet it was against the Prussians that this country fought?"

"That is so," returned his dragoman; "there were many who drew attention to the fact. And at the conclusion of the Great Skirmish the reaction was such that for a long moment even the leader-writers wavered in their self-less doctrines; nor could continuity be secured till the Laborious Party came solidly to the saddle in 1930. Since then the principle has been firm but the practice has been firmer, and public morality has never been altogether superlative. Let us pass to comparative public morality. In the days of the Great Skirmish this was practised by those with names, who told others what to do. This large and capable body included all the preachers, publicists, and politicians of the day, and in many cases there is even evidence that they would have been willing to practise what they preached if their age had not been so venerable or their directive power so invaluable."

"*In*-valuable," murmured the Angel; "has that word a negative significa-tion?"

"Not in all cases," said his dragoman with a smile; "there were men whom it would have been difficult to replace, though not many, and those perhaps the least comparatively moral. In this category, too, were undoubt-edly the persons known as conchies."

"From conch, a shell?" asked the Angel.

"Not precisely," returned his dragoman; "and yet you have hit it, sir, for into their shells they certainly withdrew, refusing to have anything to do with this wicked world. Sufficient unto them was the voice within. They were not well treated by an unfeeling populace."

"This is interesting to me," said the Angel. "To what did they object?"

"To war," replied his dragoman. "'What is it to us,' they said, 'that there should be barbarians like these Prussians, who override the laws of justice and humanity?'—words, sir, very much in vogue in those days. 'How can it effect our principles if these rude foreigners have not our views, and are prepared, by cutting off the food supplies of this island, to starve us into sub-mission to their rule? Rather than turn a deaf ear to the voice within we are prepared for general starvation; whether we are prepared for the starvation of our individual selves we cannot, of course, say until we experience it. But we hope for the best, and believe that we shall go through with it to death, in the undesired company of all who do not agree with us.' And it is certain, sir, that some of them were capable of this; for there is, as you know, a type of man who will die rather than admit that his views are too extreme to keep himself and his fellow-men alive."

"How entertaining!" said the Angel. "Do such persons still exist?"

"Oh! yes," replied the dragoman; "and always will. Nor is it, in my opin-ion, altogether to the disadvantage of mankind, for they afford a salutary warning to the human species not to isolate itself in fancy from the realities of existence and extinguish human life before its time has come. We shall now consider the positively moral. At the time of the Great Skirmish these were such as took no sugar in their tea and invested all they had in War Stock at five per cent. without waiting for what were called Premium Bonds to be issued. They were a large and healthy group, more immediately concerned with commerce than the war. But the largest body of all were the negatively moral. These were they who did what they crudely called 'their bit,' which I may tell you, sir, was often very bitter. I myself was a ship's steward at the time, and frequently swallowed much salt water, owing to the submarines. But I was not to be deterred, and would sign on again when it had been pumped out of me. Our morality was purely negative, if not actually low. We acted, as it were, from instinct, and often wondered at the sublime sacrifices which were being made by our betters. Most of us were killed or injured in one way or another; but a blind and obstinate mania for not giving in possessed us. We were a simple lot." The dragoman paused and fixed his eyes on the empty hearth. "I will not disguise from you," he added "that we were fed-up nearly all the time; and yet—we couldn't stop. Odd, was it not?"

"I wish I had been with you," said the Angel, "for—to use that word without which you English seem unable to express anything—you were heroes."

"Sir," said his dragoman, "you flatter us by such encomium. We were, I fear, dismally lacking in commercial spirit, just men and women in the street having neither time nor inclination to examine our conduct and motives, nor to question or direct the conduct of others. Purely negative beings, with perhaps a touch of human courage and human kindliness in us. All this, however, is a tale of long ago. You can now ask me any questions, sir, before I pass to private morality."

"You allude to courage and kindliness," said the Angel: "How do these qualities now stand?"

"The quality of courage," responded his dragoman, "received a set-back in men's estimation at the time of the Great Skirmish, from which it has never properly recovered. For physical courage was then, for the first time, perceived to be most excessively common; it is, indeed, probably a mere attribute of the bony chin, especially prevalent in the English-speaking races. As to moral courage, it was so hunted down that it is still somewhat in hiding. Of kindliness there are, as you know, two sorts: that which people manifest towards their own belongings; and that which they do not as a rule manifest towards every one else."

"Since we attended the Divorce Court," remarked the Angel with deliberation, "I have been thinking. And I fancy no one can be really kind unless they have had matrimonial trouble, preferably in conflict with the law."

"A new thought to me," observed his dragoman attentively; "and yet you may be right, for there is nothing like being morally outcast to make you feel the intolerance of others. But that brings us to private morality."

"Quite!" said the Angel, with relief. "I forgot to ask you this morning how the ancient custom of marriage was now regarded in the large?"

"Not indeed as a sacrament," replied his dragoman; "such a view was becoming rare already at the time of the Great Skirmish. Yet the notion might have been preserved but for the opposition of the Pontifical of those days to the reform of the Divorce Laws. When principle opposes common sense too long, a landslide follows."

"Of what nature, then, is marriage now?"

"Purely a civil, or uncivil, contract, as the case may be. The holy state of judicial separation, too, has long been unknown."

"Ah!" said the Angel, "that was the custom by which the man became a monk and the lady a nun, was it not?"

"In theory, sir," replied his dragoman, "but in practice not a little bit, as you may well suppose. The Pontifical, however, and the women, old and otherwise, who supported them, had but small experience of life to go on, and honestly believed that they were punishing those still-married but erring persons who were thus separated. These, on the contrary, almost invariably assumed that they were justified in free companionships, nor were they particular to avoid promiscuity! So it ever is, sir, when the great laws of Nature are violated in deference to the Higher Doctrine."

"Are children still-born out of wedlock?" asked the Angel.

"Yes," said his dragoman, "but no longer considered responsible for the past conduct of their parents."

"Society, then, is more humane?"

"Well, sir, we shall not see the Millennium in that respect for some years to come. Zoos are still permitted, and I read only yesterday a letter from a Scottish gentleman pouring scorn on the humane proposal that prisoners should be allowed to see their wives once a month without bars or the presence of a third party; precisely as if we still lived in the days of the Great Skirmish. Can you tell me why it is that such letters are always written by Scotsmen?"

"Is it a riddle?" asked the Angel.

"It is indeed, sir."

"Then it bores me. Speaking generally, are you satisfied with current virtue now that it is a State matter, as you informed me yesterday?"

"To tell you the truth, sir, I do not judge my neighbours; sufficient unto myself is the vice thereof. But one thing I observe, the less virtuous people assume themselves to be, the more virtuous they commonly are. Where the lime-light is not, the flower blooms. Have you not frequently noticed that they who day by day cheerfully endure most unpleasant things, while helping their neighbours at the expense of their own time and goods, are often rendered lyrical by receiving a sovereign from some one who would never miss it, and are ready to enthrone him in their hearts as a king of men? The truest virtue, sir, must be sought among the lowly. Sugar and snow may be seen on the top, but for the salt of the earth one must look to the bottom."

"I believe you," said the Angel. "It is probably harder for a man in the lime-light to enter virtue than for the virtuous to enter the lime-light. Ha, ha! Is the good old custom of buying honour still preserved?"

"No, sir; honour is now only given to such as make themselves too noisy to be endured, and saddles the recipient with an obligation to preserve public silence for a period not exceeding three years. That maximum sentence is given for a dukedom. It is reckoned that few can survive so fearful a term."

"Concerning the morality of this new custom," said the Angel, "I feel doubtful. It savours of surrender to the bully and the braggart, does it not?"

"Rather to the bore, sir; not necessarily the same thing. But whether men be decorated for making themselves useful, or troublesome, the result in either case is to secure a comparative inertia, which has ever been the desideratum; for you must surely be aware, sir, how a man's dignity weighs him down."

"Are women also rewarded in this way?"

"Yes, and very often; for although their dignity is already ample, their tongues are long, and they have little shame and no nerves in the matter of public speaking."

"And what price their virtue?" asked the Angel.

"There is some change since the days of the Great Skirmish," responded his dragoman. "They do not now so readily sell it, except for a wedding-ring; and many marry for love. Women, indeed, are often deplorably lacking in commercial spirit; and though they now mix in commerce, have not yet been able to adapt themselves. Some men even go so far as to think that their participation in active life is not good for trade and keeps the country back."

"They are a curious sex," said the Angel; "I like them, but they make too much fuss about babies."

"Ah! sir; there is the great flaw. The mother instinct—so heedless and uncommercial! They seem to love the things just for their own sakes."

"Yes," said the Angel, "there's no future in it. Give me a cigar."

VIII

"What, then, is the present position of 'the good'?" asked the Angel Æthereal, taking wing from Watchester Cathedrome towards the City Tabernacle.

"There are a number of discordant views, sir," his dragoman whiffled through his nose in the rushing air; "which is no more novel in this year of Peace 1947 than it was when you were here in 1910. On the far right are certain extremists, who believe it to be what it was—omnipotent, but suffering the presence of 'the bad' for no reason which has yet been ascertained; omnipresent, though presumably absent where 'the bad' is present; mysterious, though perfectly revealed; terrible, though loving; eternal, though limited by a beginning and an end. They are not numerous, but all stall-holders, and chiefly characterised by an almost perfect intolerance of those whose views do not coincide with their own; nor will they suffer for a moment any examination into the nature of 'the good,' which they hold to be established for all time, in the form I have stated, by persons who have long been dead. They are, as you may imagine, somewhat out of touch with science, such as it is, and are regarded by the community at large rather with curiosity than anything else."

"The type is well known in the sky," said the Angel. "Tell me: Do they torture those who do not agree with them?"

"Not materially," responded his dragoman. "Such a custom was extinct even before the days of the Great Skirmish, though what would have happened if the Patriotic or Prussian Party had been able to keep power for any length of time we cannot tell. As it is, the torture they apply is purely spiritual, and consists in looking down their noses at all who have not their belief and calling them erratics. But it would be a mistake to underrate their power, for human nature loves the Pontifical, and there are those who will follow to the death any one who looks down his nose, and says: 'I know!' Moreover, sir, consider how unsettling a question 'the good' is, when you come to think about it and how unfatiguing the faith which precludes all such speculation."

"That is so," said the Angel thoughtfully.

"The right centre," continued his dragoman, "is occupied by the small yet noisy Fifth Party. These are they who play the cornet and tambourine, big drum and concertina, descendants of the Old Prophet, and survivors of those who, following a younger prophet, joined them at the time of the Great Skirmish. In a form ever modifying with scientific discovery they hold that 'the good' is a superman, bodiless yet bodily, with a beginning but without an end. It is an attractive faith, enabling them to say to Nature: '*Je m'en fiche de tout cela*. My big brother will look after me. Pom!' One may call it anthropomorphia, for it seems especially soothing to strong personalities. Every man to his creed, as they say; and I would never wish to throw cold water on such as seek to find 'the good' by closing one eye instead of two, as is done by the extremists on the right."

"You are tolerant," said the Angel.

"Sir," said his dragoman, "as one gets older, one perceives more and more how impossible it is for man not to regard himself as the cause of the universe, and for certain individual men not to believe themselves the centre of the cause. For such to start a new belief is a biological necessity, and should by no means be discouraged. It is a safety-valve—the form of passion which the fires of youth take in men after the age of fifty, as one may judge by the case of the prophet Tolstoy and other great ones. But to resume: In the centre, of course, are situated the enormous majority of the community, whose view is that they have no view of what 'the good' is."

"None?" repeated the Angel Æthereal, somewhat struck.

"Not the faintest," answered his dragoman. "These are the only true mystics; for what is a mystic if not one with an impenetrable belief in the mystery of his own existence? This group embraces the great bulk of the Laborious. It is true that many of them will repeat what is told them of 'the good' as if it were their own view, without compunction, but this is no more than the majority of persons have done from the beginning of time."

"Quite," admitted the Angel; "I have observed that phenomenon in the course of my travels. We will not waste words on them."

"Ah, sir!" retorted his dragoman, "there is more wisdom in these persons than you imagine. For, consider what would be the fate of their brains if they attempted to think for themselves. Moreover, as you know, all definite views about 'the good' are very wearing, and it is better, so this great majority thinks, to let sleeping dogs lie than to have them barking in its head. But I will tell you something," the dragoman added: "These innumerable persons have a secret belief of their own, old as the Greeks, that good fellowship is all that matters. And, in my opinion, taking 'the good' in its limited sense, it is an admirable creed."

"Oh! cut on!" said the Angel.

"My mistake, sir!" said his dragoman. "On the left centre are grouped that increasing section whose view is that since everything is very bad, 'the good' is ultimate extinction—'Peace, perfect peace,' as the poet says. You will recollect the old tag: 'To be or not to be.' These are they who have answered that question in the negative; pessimists masquerading to an unsuspecting public as optimists. They are no doubt descendants of such as used to be called 'Theosophians,' a sect which presupposed everything and then desired to be annihilated; or, again, of the Christian Scientites, who simply could not bear things as they were, so set themselves to think they were not, with some limited amount of success, if I remember rightly. I recall to mind the case of a lady who lost her virtue, and recovered it by dint of remembering that she had no body."

"Curious!" said the Angel. "I should like to question her; let me have her address after the lecture. Does the theory of reincarnation still obtain?"

"I do not wonder, sir, that you are interested in the point, for believers in that doctrine are compelled, by the old and awkward rule that 'Two and two make four,' to draw on other spheres for the reincarnation of their spirits."

"I do not follow," said the Angel.

"It is simple, however," answered his dragoman, "for at one time on earth, as is admitted, there was no life. The first incarnation, therefore—an amœba, we used to be told—enclosed a spirit, possibly from above. It may, indeed, have been yours, sir. Again, at some time on this earth, as is admitted, there will again be no life; the last spirit will therefore flit to an incarnation, possibly below; and again, sir, who knows, it may be yours."

"I cannot jest on such a subject," said the Angel, with a sneeze.

"No offence," murmured his dragoman. "The last group, on the far left, to which indeed I myself am not altogether unaffiliated, is composed of a small number of extremists, who hold that 'the good' is things as they are— pardon the inevitable flaw in grammar. They consider that what is now has always been, and will always be; that things do but swell and contract and swell again, and so on for ever and ever; and that, since they could not swell if they did not contract, since without the black there could not be the white, nor pleasure without pain, nor virtue without vice, nor criminals without judges; even contraction, or the black, or pain, or vice, or judges, are not 'the bad,' but only negatives; and that all is for the best in the best of all possible worlds. They are Voltairean optimists masquerading to an unsuspecting population as pessimists. 'Eternal Variation' is their motto."

"I gather," said the Angel, "that these think there is no purpose in existence?"

"Rather, sir, that existence *is* the purpose. For, if you consider, any other conception of purpose implies fulfilment, or an *end*, which they do not admit, just as they do not admit a beginning."

"How logical!" said the Angel. "It makes me dizzy! You have renounced the idea of climbing, then?"

"Not so," responded his dragoman. "We climb to the top of the pole, slide imperceptibly down, and begin over again; but since we never really know whether we are climbing or sliding, this does not depress us."

"To believe that this goes on for ever is futile," said the Angel.

"So we are told," replied his dragoman, without emotion. "*We* think, however, that the truth is with us, in spite of jesting Pilate."

"It is not for me," said the Angel with dignity, "to argue with my dragoman."

"No, sir, for it is always necessary to beware of the open mind. I myself find it very difficult to believe the same thing every day. And the fact that is whatever you believe will probably not alter the truth, which may be said to have a certain mysterious immutability, considering the number of efforts men have made to change it from time to time. We are now, however, just above the City Tabernacle, and if you will close your wings we shall penetrate it through the claptrap-door which enables its preachers now and then to ascend to higher spheres."

"Stay!" said the Angel; "let me float a minute while I suck a peppermint, for the audiences in these places often have colds." And with that delicious aroma clinging to them they made their entry through a strait gate in the roof and took their seats in the front row, below a tall prophet in eyeglasses, who was discoursing on the stars. The Angel slept heavily.

"You have lost a good thing, sir," said his dragoman reproachfully, when they left the Tabernacle.

"In my opinion," the Angel playfully responded, "I won a better, for I went nap. What can a mortal know about the stars?"

"Believe me," answered his dragoman, "the subject is not more abstruse than is generally chosen."

"If he had taken religion I should have listened with pleasure," said the Angel.

"Oh! sir, but in these days such a subject is unknown in a place of worship. Religion is now exclusively a State affair. The change began with discipline and the Education Bill in 1918, and has gradually crystallised ever since. It is true that individual extremists on the right make continual endeavours to encroach on the functions of the State, but they preach to empty houses."

"And the Deity?" said the Angel: "You have not once mentioned Him. It has struck me as curious."

"Belief in the Deity," responded his dragoman, "perished shortly after the Great Skirmish, during which there was too active and varied an effort to revive it. Action, as you know, sir, always brings reaction, and it must be said that the spiritual propaganda of those days was so grossly tinged with the commercial spirit that it came under the head of profiteering and earned for itself a certain abhorrence. For no sooner had the fears and griefs brought by the Great Skirmish faded from men's spirits than they perceived that their new impetus towards the Deity had been directed purely by the longing for protection, solace, comfort, and reward, and not by any real desire for 'the good' in itself. It was this truth, together with the appropriation of the word by Emperors, and the expansion of our towns, a process ever destructive of traditions, which brought about extinction of belief in His existence."

"It was a large order," said the Angel.

"It was more a change of nomenclature," replied his dragoman. "The ruling motive for belief in 'the good' is still the hope of getting something out of it—the commercial spirit is innate."

"Ah!" said the Angel, absently. "Can we have another lunch now? I could do with a slice of beef."

"An admirable idea, sir," replied his dragoman, "we will have it in the White City."

IX

"What in your opinion is the nature of happiness?" asked the Angel Æthereal, as he finished his second bottle of Bass, in the grounds of the White City. The dragoman regarded his angel with one eye.

"The question is not simple, sir, though often made the subject of symposiums in the more intellectual journals. Even now, in the middle of the twentieth century, some still hold that it is a by-product of fresh air and liquor. The Old and Merrie England indubitably procured it from those elements. Some, again, imagine it to follow from high thinking and low living, while no mean number believe that it depends on women."

"Their absence or their presence?" asked the Angel, with interest.

"Some this and others that. But for my part, it is not altogether the outcome of these causes."

"Is this now a happy land?"

"Sir," returned his dragoman, "all things earthly are comparative."

"Get on with it," said the Angel.

"I will comply," responded his dragoman reproachfully, "if you will permit me first to draw your third cork. And let me say in passing that even your present happiness is comparative, or possibly superlative, as you will know when you have finished this last bottle. It may or may not be greater; we shall see."

"We shall," said the Angel, resolutely.

"You ask me whether this land is happy; but must we not first decide what happiness is? And how difficult this will be you shall soon discover. For example, in the early days of the Great Skirmish, happiness was reputed nonexistent; every family was plunged into anxiety or mourning; and, though this to my own knowledge was not the case, such as were not pretended to be. Yet, strange as it may appear, the shrewd observer of those days was unable to remark any indication of added gloom. Certain creature comforts, no doubt, were scarce, but there was no lack of spiritual comfort, which high minds have ever associated with happiness; nor do I here allude to liquor. What, then, was the nature of this spiritual comfort, you will certainly be asking. I will tell you, and in seven words: People forgot themselves and remembered other people. Until those days it had never been realised what a lot of medical men could be spared from the civil population; what a number of clergymen, lawyers, stockbrokers, artists, writers, politicians, and other persons, whose work in life is to cause people to think about themselves, never would be missed. Invalids knitted socks and forgot to be unwell; old gentlemen read the papers and forgot to talk about their food; people travelled in trains and forgot not to fall into conversation with each other; merchants became special constables and forgot to differ about property; the House of Lords remembered its dignity and forgot its impudence; the House of Commons almost forgot to chatter. The case of the working-man was the most striking of all—he forgot he was the working man. The very dogs forgot themselves, though that, to be sure, was no novelty, as the Irish writer demonstrated in his terrific outburst: 'On my doorstep.' But time went on, and hens in their turn forgot to lay, ships to return to port, cows to give enough milk, and Governments to look ahead, till the first flush of self-forgetfulness which had dyed peoples' cheeks———"

"Died on them," put in the Angel, with a quiet smile.

"You take my meaning, sir," said his dragoman, "though I should not have worded it so happily. But certainly the return to self began, and people used to think: 'The war is not so bloody as I thought, for I am getting better money than I ever did; and the longer it lasts the more I shall get, and for the sake of this I am prepared to endure much.' The saying 'Beef and beer, for soon you must put up the shutters,' became the motto of all classes. 'If I am to be shot, drowned, bombed, ruined, or starved tomorrow,' they said, 'I had better eat, drink, marry, and buy jewellery today.' And so they did, in spite of the dreadful efforts of one bishop and two gentlemen who presided over the important question of food. They did not, it is true, relax their manual efforts to accomplish the defeat of their enemies or 'win the war,' as it was somewhat loosely called; but they no longer worked with their spirits, which, with a few exceptions, went to sleep. For, sir, the spirit, like the body, demands regular repose, and in my opinion is usually the first of the two to snore. Before the Great Skirmish came at last to its appointed end the snoring from spirits in this country might have been heard in the moon. People thought of little but money, revenge, and what they could get to eat, though the word 'sacrifice' was so accustomed to their lips that they could no more get it off them than the other forms of lip-salve, increasingly in vogue. They became very merry. And the question I would raise is this: By which of these two standards shall we assess the word 'happiness'? Were these people happy when they mourned and thought not of self; or when they married and thought of self all the time?"

"By the first standard," replied the Angel, with kindling eyes. "Happiness is undoubtedly nobility."

"Not so fast, sir," replied his dragoman; "for I have frequently met with nobility in distress; and, indeed, the more exalted and refined the mind, the unhappier is frequently the owner thereof, for to him are visible a thousand cruelties and mean injustices which lower natures do not perceive."

"Hold!" exclaimed the Angel: "This is blasphemy against Olympus, 'The Spectator,' and other High-Brows."

"Sir," replied his dragoman gravely, "I am not one of those who accept gilded doctrines without examination; I read in the Book of Life rather than in the million tomes written by men to get away from their own unhappiness."

"I perceive," said the Angel, with a shrewd glance, "that you have something up your sleeve. Shake it out!"

"My conclusion is this, sir," returned his dragoman, well pleased: "Man is only happy when he is living at a certain pressure of life to the square inch; in other words, when he is so absorbed in what he is doing, making, saying, thinking, or dreaming, that he has lost self-consciousness. If there be upon him any ill—such as toothache or moody meditation—so poignant as to prevent him losing himself in the interest of the moment, then he is not happy. Nor must he merely think himself absorbed, but actually be so, as are two lovers sitting under one umbrella, or he who is just making a couplet rhyme."

"Would you say then," insinuated the Angel, "that a man is happy when he meets a mad bull in a narrow lane? For there will surely be much pressure of life to the square inch."

"It does not follow," responded his dragoman; "for at such moments one is prone to stand apart, pitying himself and reflecting on the unevenness of fortune. But if he collects himself and meets the occasion with spirit he will enjoy it until, while sailing over the hedge, he has leisure to reflect once more. It is clear to me," he proceeded, "that the fruit of the tree of knowledge in the old fable was not, as has hitherto been supposed by a puritanical people, the mere knowledge of sex, but symbolised rather general self-consciousness; for I have little doubt that Adam and Eve sat together under one umbrella long before they discovered they had no clothes on. Not until they became self-conscious about things at large did they become unhappy."

"Love is commonly reputed by some, and power by others, to be the keys of happiness," said the Angel, regardless of his grammar.

"Duds," broke in his dragoman. "For love and power are only two of the various paths to absorption, or unconsciousness of self; mere methods by which men of differing natures succeed in losing their self-consciousness, for he who, like Saint Francis, loves all creation, has no time to be conscious of loving himself, and he who rattles the sword and rules like Bill Kaser, has no time to be conscious that he is not ruling himself. I do not deny that such men may be happy, but not because of the love or the power. No, it is because they are loving or ruling with such intensity that they forget themselves in doing it."

"There is much in what you say," said the Angel thoughtfully. "How do you apply it to the times and land in which you live?"

"Sir," his dragoman responded, "the Englishman never has been, and is not now, by any means so unhappy as he looks, for, where you see a furrow in the brow, or a mouth a little open, it portends absorption rather than thoughtfulness—unless, indeed, it means adenoids—and is the mark of a naturally self-forgetful nature; nor should you suppose that poverty and dirt which abound, as you see, even under the sway of the Laborious, is necessarily deterrent to the power of living in the moment; it may even be a symptom of that habit. The unhappy are more frequently the clean and leisured, especially in times of peace, when they have little to do save sit under mulberry trees, invest money, pay their taxes, wash, fly, and think about themselves. Nevertheless, many of the Laborious also live at half-cock, and cannot be said to have lost consciousness of self."

"Then democracy is not synonymous with happiness?" asked the Angel.

"Dear sir," replied his dragoman, "I know they said so at the time of the Great Skirmish. But they said so much that one little one like that hardly counted. I will let you into a secret. We have not yet achieved democracy, either here or anywhere else. The old American saying about it is all very well, but since not one man in ten has any real opinion of his own on any subject on which he votes, he cannot, with the best will in the world, put it on record. Not until he learns to have and record his own real opinion will he truly govern himself for himself, which is, as you know, the test of true democracy?"

"I am getting fuddled," said the Angel. "What is it you want to make you happy?"

His dragoman sat up: "If I am right," he purred, "in my view that happiness is absorption, our problem is to direct men's minds to absorption in right and pleasant things. An American making a corner in wheat is absorbed and no doubt happy, yet he is an enemy of mankind, for his activity is destructive. We should seek to give our minds to creation, to activities good for others as well as for ourselves, to simplicity, pride in work, and forgetfulness of self in every walk of life. We should do things for the sheer pleasure of doing them, and not for what they may or may not be going to bring us in, and be taught always to give our whole minds to it; in this way only will the edge of our appetite for existence remain as keen as a razor which is stropped every morning by one who knows how. On the negative side we should be brought up to be kind, to be clean, to be moderate, and to love good music, exercise, and fresh air."

"That sounds a bit of all right," said the Angel. "What measures are being taken in these directions?"

"It has been my habit, sir, to study the Education Acts of my country ever since that which was passed at the time of the Great Skirmish; but, with the exception of exercise, I have not as yet been able to find any direct allusion to these matters. Nor is this surprising when you consider that education is popularly supposed to be, not for the acquisition of happiness, but for the good of trade or the promotion of acute self-consciousness through what we know as culture. If by any chance there should arise a President of Education so enlightened as to share my views, it would be impossible for him to mention the fact for fear of being sent to Colney Hatch."

"In that case," asked the Angel, "you do not believe in the progress of your country?"

"Sir," his dragoman replied earnestly, "you have seen this land for yourself and have heard from me some account of its growth from the days when you were last on earth, shortly before the Great Skirmish; it will not have escaped your eagle eye that this considerable event has had some influence in accelerating the course of its progression; and you will have noticed how, notwithstanding the most strenuous intentions at the close of that tragedy, we have yielded to circumstance and in every direction followed the line of least resistance."

"I have a certain sympathy with that," said the Angel, with a yawn; "it is so much easier."

"So we have found; and our country has got along, perhaps, as well as one could have expected, considering what it has had to contend with: pressure of debt; primrose paths; pelf; party; patrio-Prussianism; the people; pundits; Puritans; proctors; property; philosophers; the Pontifical; and progress. I will not disguise from you, however, that we are far from perfection; and it may be that on your next visit, thirty-seven years hence, we shall be further. For, however it may be with angels, sir, with men things do not stand still; and, as I have tried to make clear to you, in order to advance in body and spirit, it is necessary to be masters of your environment and discoveries instead of letting them be masters of you. Wealthy again we may be, healthy and happy we are not, as yet."

"I have finished my beer," said the Angel Æthereal with finality, "and am ready to rise. You have nothing to drink! Let me give you a testimonial instead!" Pulling a quill from his wing, he dipped it in the mustard and wrote: "A Dry Dog—No Good For Trade" on his dragoman's white hat. "I shall now leave the earth," he added.

"I am pleased to hear it," said his dragoman, "for I fancy that the longer you stay the more vulgar you will become. I have noticed it growing on you, sir, just as it does on us."

The Angel smiled. "Meet me by sunlight alone," he said, "under the left-hand lion in Trafalgar Square at this hour of this day, in 1984. Remember me to the waiter, will you? So long!" And, without pausing for a reply, he spread his wings, and soared away.

"*L'homme moyen sensuel! Sic itur ad astra!*" murmured his dragoman enigmatically, and, lifting his eyes, he followed the Angel's flight into the empyrean.